LAZER DROID
by
Derrick J. Truesdale

To My Brother Eric,
don't ever feel you are alone.

No one can ever make you feel inferior, without your consent.
— Eleanor Roosevelt

PROLOGUE

IN BALTIMORE, MARYLAND 1986, Henry and Patrice Linard sat nervously in the pediatrician's office with their four -year-old son Daryl as the boy held a 'Computer World' magazine and appeared to be reading it with the focus of an educated adult.

The exam room was smaller than the waiting area, enclosed and quietly intimate.

After the doctor entered, the door closed with a soft click, muting the distant sounds of phones and murmured voices outside.

Overhead, the lights were bright but diffused, softened by a pale plastic cover which kept the room from feeling harsh.

The walls were painted a gentle blue, faded in places from years of disinfectant wipes, and decorated with cheerful posters which explained bones and organs using smiling cartoon figures.

One corner hosted a height chart shaped like a giraffe, its paint chipped near the bottom where countless shoes have scuffed the wall.

A faint scent of antiseptic lingered, clean and sharp, layered beneath something sweeter, bubblegum or cotton candy, meant to make the space feel less intimidating.

Against the wall which was perpendicular to the door sat the exam table, narrow and crinkling beneath its paper covering, which was printed with tiny rockets drifting between stars.

A step stool rested beside it, metal legs cool and scuffed, waiting for small feet.

The paper rustled at the slightest movement, loud in the otherwise quiet room.

Against another wall opposite the door, beige cabinets remained firmly shut, their contents hidden away.

Only the basics were visible: a blood pressure cuff hanging from a hook, an otoscope resting in its cradle, a box of gloves tucked neatly beside a digital thermometer.

Everything appeared organized, controlled, nothing at all threatening, but nothing fully comforting either.

Sitting in a couple of chairs positioned next to the door, the Linards just stared at their son who, while sitting up on the exam table, remained oblivious to their gazes.

Now sitting on a rolling chair, Doctor Francis Martin, stared at the child and smiled as the boy turned the page and happened upon a picture of a black Kawasaki Ninja motorcycle with a man riding it wearing black leather pants, a black leather jacket and a matching black helmet.

Doctor Martin looked like someone who had been a doctor for a very long time and who loved every year of it.

His hair, now was silvered and neatly combed, thinning just enough to suggest experience rather than age, and his face was lined with the soft creases of someone who smiled often. His eyes were warm and attentive behind rectangular glasses, the kind which seemed to notice small things: a nervous fidget, a hesitant glance, a question someone was afraid to ask. When he smiled, it was unhurried and genuine, as though he had all the time in the world.

Martin wore a white coat which had clearly been lived in, not stiff or pristine, but comfortable, its pockets heavy with pens, a small flashlight, and folded notes. Beneath it, his shirt was simple, paired with a tie patterned with tiny animals, chosen less for fashion than for the way children's eyes light up when they noticed it. A stethoscope rested around his neck; the metal dulled from years of use.

When he spoke, his voice was calm and reassuring, carrying a gentle humor which turned fear into curiosity. He knelt instead of towering, listened instead of rushing, and explained things as if they were stories rather than instructions. There was an easy kindness in the way he moved, careful, patient, and practiced.

His presence felt familiar, like a trusted teacher or a favorite neighbor. The kind of doctor who made the room feel safer simply by being in it, and who children remembered long after they've outgrown the exam table.

"Daryl?" inquired Doctor Martin as the child looked over at him. "You seemed to be heavy into that magazine?"

Daryl smiled.

"Can you tell me what you're looking at?" Martin asked.

Daryl turned the magazine around and showed the picture of the motorcycle to Doctor Martin.

"I was just looking at this motorcycle," started Daryl. "I like motorcycles!"

Doctor Martin smiled and looked at Henry and Patrice who looked back at him. "I really don't think you have anything to..."

"But prior to looking at this bike," interrupted Daryl "I was reading how the partnership between both Steve Jobs and Steve Wozniak ended last year when Steve Jobs resigned from Apple Computers leaving many analysts to think the company would lose its footing in the tech world. But after calculating the various directions this move will make in the tech world, I believe the analyst are wrong and further predict that Steve Jobs will one day return to Apple and help promote the success of the company."

Doctor Martin sat there staring at Daryl with his mouth hanging open as his parents looked at each other and then back at the doctor.

"This is what we were talking about Doctor Martin," started Mr. Linard. "I am in no way an expert on children, but at four years old, I feel he is way more advanced than people I know who my age are."

Doctor Martin looked back over at Daryl who had already put his eyes back into the magazine. "Daryl, would you mind going to sit in the lobby with the nice lady while I talk with your parents for a moment?"

"The receptionist?" asked Daryl.

Doctor Martin smiled. "Yes, the receptionist."

Daryl held up the magazine. "Can I take this in there with me?" he asked.

"Sure you can," replied Doctor Martin as he looked at Mrs. Linard. "Can you please take him out to our receptionist and come back? He'll be okay," he added before she could protest.

Daryl soon hopped off of the table via use of the foot stool and grabbed his mother's hand while keeping a finger in the magazine at the last page he was looking at.

Dr. Martin and Mr. Linard both smiled as they watched them walk out of the door and closing it afterwards.

A minute later Mrs. Linard returned and closed the door behind her.

"This is incredible!" exclaimed Doctor Martin.

"At first we thought so too," started Mrs. Linard, but after hearing about something called autism..."

"That is not what this is," interrupted Doctor Martin.

"How can you be so sure?" asked Mr. Linard.

"I have been watching him the whole time the three of you have been sitting there," started Martin, "no repetitive motions, he doesn't appear to be socially awkward, and his diction is damn near perfect. Mrs. Linard, do you find it difficult to get a hug from him or does he hug you too much?"

"No, on either account" she replied.

"Mr. Linard, are you able to engage him in play time?"

"He loves to play games, watch cartoons on Saturday morning, all that stuff," started Mr. Linard. "We're just concerned 'cause he's surpassing so many developmental milestones rather early and we didn't want him to be singled out or have problems as he gets older."

"Then talk to him," started Doctor Martin. "It's already apparent he'll have no problem comprehending what you are saying. The questions I asked earlier are related to symptoms they have been finding in children who have autism, but if there are no concerns, and I don't believe there are, let him be. When he gets older and starts school, make sure he maintains his pace with the other students, never encourage him to dumb it down, just tell him not to move so fast."

He stood now. "Sometimes skipping grades can cause children to not fully mature or socialize appropriately, so we want him to have as much of a normal life as possible."

The Linards looked at each other and smiled.

Henry stood up followed by Patrice as he extended his hand to Doctor Martin. "Thank you so much Doctor Martin," he said as they shook hands.

"Awe, no problem at all," started Doctor Martin, "It's natural for parents to worry about the development of their children. Now let's get him back in here so we can finish his physical exam."

***

The Linard house sat close to the street, its dark red brick dulled by decades of rain. A short run of concrete steps climbed from the sidewalk to a narrow front porch, where a metal railing flaked black paint and sang softly when the wind passed through it.

Inside the home, the air was close and comforting, heavy with the promise of a home-cooked dinner. The rooms were narrow, ceilings low enough to hold in sound and heat, and the carpet pressed flat along the walking paths, springier at the edges where feet rarely wandered.

The living room was the pride of the house. A wide brown sofa stretched along one wall, its cushions firm and slightly shiny with use. Across from it stood the television, big, boxy, and housed in a wooden cabinet. Rabbit-ear antennas rose from its back like bent elbows. A lace doily rested on top, careful and decorative, beneath framed photographs of smiling relatives caught forever in Sunday clothes.

Heavy curtains framed the front window, drawn just enough to let the afternoon light in without inviting the street to stare. On the walls hung reminders of faith and family, a portrait of a gentle-eyed Jesus, a framed wedding photograph already soft at the corners, a clock which ticked louder than it should have. Toys hid beneath the coffee table, their bright plastic colors peeking out like secrets, and the television screen bore faint fingerprints where a small boy had pressed too close.

Beyond the living room, the dining room waited in quiet order. A solid wooden table filled most of the space, its surface protected by a vinyl. The chairs didn't quite match anymore, but they all knew their places. Against the wall stood a China cabinet, its glass doors guarding dishes which came out only for holidays and company, and glasses which caught the light but rarely tasted it.

A calendar hung nearby, pages curling as the months passed, and above it a photograph of their son beamed proudly from a frame, grinning, dressed too neatly for an ordinary day.

The house held their lives gently. It remembered first steps and arguments, prayers whispered late at night, laughter which spilled from room to room. It wasn't large, and it wasn't new, but it stood firm, sheltering a family doing their best to build something lasting within its walls.

Later that evening, as Daryl and his parents were sitting at the dining room table eating, Henry Linard glanced at Patrice Linard and she nodded her head in the affirmative, signaling, *yes, it is time.*

"Daryl," started Henry as his son looked up at him while still chewing his food. "We want to talk to you about the appointment today."

Daryl swallowed his food. "This has something to do with me being so smart, right?"

"Yes," replied Henry.

"We don't want you to think there's anything wrong with you," reassured Patrice.

"But there is," interrupted Daryl, "I was able to run a self-diagnostic on myself and have figured out the issue."

"I'm sorry," started Henry as he dropped his fork onto his plate. "What?!"

"The easiest way for me to explain it is, I have this small blue laser light encoded within my D-N-A. It's not confined to one area, it is able to traverse my entire body, every molecule." Daryl held up his right hand and a small blue light the size of a golf ball jumped from the right hand, and he raised the left hand to catch it and the light vanished.

Patrice gasped as her and her husband both jumped slightly back.

"I don't know where the light came from or how it came to be, but it's a part of me and I believe it is part of the reason I am able to process information the way I can."

Henry and Patrice looked at each other.

"Son," started Henry, "it's obvious right now you have an incredible gift, but please understand this, if knowledge of this gets out, I'm afraid people will try to take you away from us and experiment on you or try to make you into some type of weapon. Is there anyway, you can suppress this part of you until maybe you're in high school or even until you're an adult?"

Daryl looked at the both of them and thought about it for a few seconds. "Your hypothesis sounds logical...yes, if it will make you both happy and you feel doing so will keep me safe, I can instruct Crystal to block my processors and that portion of my data cells in such a way as to dial back my intellect and reasoning, at least until I truly need those skills."

"Crystal?" asked Patrice.

"The blue laser light," started Daryl as he picked his fork up and took another bite of food. "That's her name!"

Henry shook his head in the affirmative.

Daryl put down his fork and closed his eyes briefly as his parents stared at him intently.

Even with his eyes closed you could see them fluttering as if he were processing data.

After a few moments, Daryl opened his eyes and smiled.

"Is it done?" asked Henry.

"I liked being smart," started Daryl, "but in thirty seconds, I will learn new information at the correct developmental rate, and my laser light will stay still for a while holding back my memory and that part of me which is...too technical, I will just need you two to remind me about my gift later by having me say the name I told you earlier."

"Crystal?" asked Patrice.

"Yes, you have the key and with it, I will be fully unlocked," replied Daryl.

Tell them their deaths will unlock you also!

"I'm not telling them that!" exclaimed Daryl under his breath.

Henry and Patrice smiled and looked at each other and then worriedly back at their toddler. They then smiled and nodded in the affirmative.

Five.

Four.

"Thank you, baby," said Patrice.

Three.

Two.

Daryl smiled.

One.

Blue lights glossed briefly over his eyes.

"Tomorrow, can we go to the slide at the outside park?" asked Daryl.

Henry and Patrice both laughed with joy as a tear came to Patrice Linards' eye.

Their little boy was already starting to sound like the toddler he was supposed to be.

"You want to go where?" asked Henry, just to hear him say it again.

"To the slide," repeated Daryl, "at the outside park...the playground!"

Of course we can baby," said Patrice smilingly as Henry picked up his fork smilingly and continued to eat.

"Of course we can!"

ONE

Twenty-five years later...

THE LIGHTENING FLASH illuminated the heavy rain pouring down as the deafening thunder echoed through the sky.

Daryl Linard, a seasoned truck driver of ten years, gripped the steering wheel tightly, his eyes fixed on the road ahead, even though the veil of water attempted with little effort to obscure his vision.

The wind continued to howl, while also causing the trees to sway swiftly violently from left to right, as he navigated through the storm steadily along interstate three seventy-six.

Despite the challenging conditions, Daryl remained calm and focused, determined to reach his destination.

KRAKOW!

Another loud crack of thunder shook the truck, unnerving Daryl as he pressed on.

He couldn't see any lightning, but the thunder seemed to be getting closer. His heart raced as he wondered if he should pull over and wait out the storm. His employer claimed many times that pulling over wasn't an option, not when he had delivery deadlines to meet.

He pressed on, his wipers working overtime to clear his view of the road.

Each passing mile felt like an eternity as the storm raged on.

Rain continued to hammer the windshield, the wipers barely keeping up as thunder continue to roll somewhere too close for comfort.

Daryl reached over and keyed the mic.

"Dispatch, this is Linard, unit twenty-forty-six. I'm on three-seventy-six westbound and this storm is getting ugly real fast."

A burst of static answered him, then a familiar voice.

"Copy that, twenty-forty-six. We're seeing the weather band moving through your area now. How's visibility?"

"Bad. Wind's kicking the trailer side to side, rain's coming down sideways. Feels like the road's disappearing in front of me."

There was a brief pause, papers shifting, keys clicking.

"Alright. Official protocol says keep moving if it's safe, but listen to me, Daryl, don't push it. Deadlines don't matter if you don't make it home."

Daryl let out a breath he didn't realize he'd been holding.

"Appreciate that. I'll slow it down a bit."

Thunder cracked so loud it rattled the cab.

"We trust your judgment. Just keep us posted."

Daryl's eyes narrowed as his headlights caught something ahead.

"Hold on...I've got hazard lights up ahead. Looks like a car stopped cross wise in two left lanes."

He eased off the accelerator.

"You able to pass?"

"Maybe. And, uh, I've got a downed power pole. Lines are sparking across the road."

Static hissed sharply this time.

"Copy that. Do *not* exit the vehicle. Keep your distance."

Static.

"Roger that. I'm pulling up short and setting my brakes, until I feel I can safely proceed."

Another flash of lightning lit the roadway like daylight, and Daryl thought he had spotted the silhouette of someone in the stopped vehicle.

"I think someone's still in the vehicle, I'm going to check on the driver if it's safe. I've got rubber soles and I'll keep clear of the lines."

Static.

A pause.

"I would tell you not to try and play hero, but I know better."

Daryl laughed. "Glad you do!"

"Daryl... be careful."

Static.

He thumbed the mic one last time.

"Always am. I'll call back when I can."

The line went dead as the rain swallowed the sound of everything else.

Daryl soon slowed to a complete stop, and he looked again from the flashing hazard lights of the car over to the downed electric pole with sparking wires dancing in the street. He especially noted the gap of space in between the two as he thought he should be able to navigate the rig through.

He looked in both directions and saw there were no other cars in sight.

He could see the passenger's side of the vehicle and saw a woman banging on the window.

He briefly remembered the story he heard about a greenish-yellow super being in Philadelphia. "Where's a superhero when you need one?" he asked out loud and to himself.

Daryl then put the semi-truck in park. He reached over the doghouse into the floor area of the passenger's seat and grabbed a pair of thick rubber soled galoshes.

After removing the Timberlands he had on, he donned the galoshes and grabbed his yellow raincoat with the reflective trim, in case other vehicles were to approach.

Daryl then carefully got out of the truck and made his way over to the car.

Even though they were a good distance from the sparking wires, he made sure to be careful with how he traversed the roadway.

As he finally made it to the passenger's door, he signaled the woman to roll the window down.

She complied as some of the rain immediately began to hit her face and she removed her glasses.

"DARYL!" he yelled

"DOCTOR JENNIFER HARDING!"

"WHAT HAPPENED TO YOUR CAR?" he asked, continuing to yell over natures' loud roar.

She huffed and reciprocated. "NOT SURE," she started, "THE CAR SHUT OFF. MY BATTERY'S STILL WORKING BUT FOR SOME REASON, I'M GETTING THIS CLICKING NOISE AND THE CAR WON'T TURN OVER!"

Daryl nodded in the affirmative. "SOUND'S LIKE YOUR ALTERNATOR! IT'S GOING TO DRAIN YOUR BATTERY TOO! I CAN TAKE YOU TO THE NEXT SERVICE STATION WHICH IS ABOUT SEVEN MILES DOWN THE ROAD. YOU SHOULD BE

ABLE TO GET HELP THERE, AND I THINK THERE IS A HO-TEL ON THE SAME STRIP!"

"THERE IS!" she agreed as she quickly wiped the water off of her face. "I LIVE IN THE AREA BUT WAS ACTUALLY HEADED TO THE HOTEL AFTER MY PRESENTATION TO-NIGHT. DUMB LUCK HUH?"

Daryl nodded in the affirmative. "THERE ARE WIRES DOWN IN THE STREET OVER THERE, YOU WERE SMART NOT TO GET OUT!"

"I ACTUALLY WORK WITH ELECTRICITY!" she laughed. "YOU WOULD THINK I WOULD HAVE HAD BETTER LUCK!"

"I HAVE ON RUBBER SOLED BOOTS, WHEN YOU OPEN THE DOOR, I'M GOING TO CARRY YOU OVER TO MY TRUCK WHERE YOU'LL GET IN THROUGH THE DRIVERS SIDE AND CLIMB OVER!"

"YES! THANK YOU!" She grabbed her purse out of the pas-senger's seat and Daryl reached in and effortlessly scooped her out of the car as the rain continued to pour down forcefully on them.

"BY THE WAY," she started as he moved back towards his rig. "BEING GROUNDED WITH RUBBER SOLES IS A MYTH, PURE VOLTAGE FROM LIGHTENING IS MUCH HIGHER THAN SAY ..."

"DOWNED SPARKING WIRES," he interrupted.

Lightening flashed a few yards from them as he hurriedly continued crossing the street with her in his arms.

KRAKOW!

Another sound of thunder crashing through the sky and then without warning, a lightning bolt struck them both a few feet from the truck, knocking them onto the ground.

Everything went dark for both of them.

The rain continued to pour down onto their motionless bod-ies.

TWO

HERITAGE VALLEY HOSPITAL had a parking lot which saw its fair share of activity last night, and the talk was about the two people brought in through the emergency department, both struck by lightning, one with life threatening bodily damage and needing emergency surgery.

The other with no apparent injury, but just in a state of unconsciousness for a few hours, found to be stable, and sent to a room on their medical-surgical unit.

Daryl Linard still lay asleep in recovery and would soon be transferred to a room.

Outside in the waiting room, Daryl's mother and father stood up as they saw the hospitalist come out into the waiting area.

Doctor Stephen Zuckerman was an older man with white hair and matching full beard. He was tall, standing at six feet two inches, and a little stout. He removed his kippah from his head and held it in front of him as he approached the couple.

"Dr. Zuckerman, how did the surgeries go?" asked Patrice Linard with anxiousness dressing her words.

"He's going to be fine," started Doctor Zuckerman, "but he isn't out of the woods yet. He's been wake...in and out of sleep actually, aware of his amputations, but he's pretty calm so I don't think it hit him yet. He will be dealing with the shock of losing both his left arm and his right leg."

Henry Linard shook his head in the negative as he hugged his wife who cried.

"Following psychological therapy, we have a special team of orthopedic surgeons who have been working with the prosthetics division of Helix Systems, they performed the surgeries as well as measured him for the prosthetics.

They will meet with you and go over everything you all discussed prior regarding pain management, the radical prosthetic treatment your son will be receiving including his fittings, their designs and how they work, what his occupational and physical therapy will look like, after proper prosthetic fitting...and you'll be happy to learn he can still lead a productive and normal life."

"I hear what you're saying doc," started Henry, "but our boy is a truck driver and a mechanic, and he loves to ride his motorcycle in his free time, how are we going to tell him he can't do those things anymore?"

"By not focusing on the things he can't do and focusing on the things he can do," Zuckerman replied solemnly. "He's going to need a lot of support and encouragement from you, both of you!"

"When can we see him?" asked Patrice.

"Well, he'll be transferred from our PACU to one of our exclusive rooms," started Zuckerman as he reapplied his kippah. "As soon as we know the exact room number, we will provide that to you, and you will be welcome to wait there until he is brought up!"

Patrice looked at her husband and then back at the doctor. "I'm not sure if his insurance will cover..."

Zuckerman threw up his hand interrupting her, "Mrs. Linard, your son risked his life and literally his limbs to save someone. Your son is a hero...and here at Heritage Valley, we will treat him as such! Everything is fully covered!"

Henry extended his hand to the surgeon who took it immediately, shaking it. "Thank you for all you've done for our boy," He said.

Zuckerman nodded in the affirmative and then shook Patrices' hand before he walked off.

Henry then walked back towards his seat, but his wife stopped him.

"Maybe we can meet this woman he saved?" she suggested.

***

The large hospital room in which Jennifer Harding was in accommodated two guests, one of which she was.

Her bed was closest to the door, and a thin curtain was drawn between hers and her roommate's bed.

There was a window next to the door, and she had a good view of the nurse's station which was catty-cornered from her field of vision.

On the same side as the room door was a closet which sat across from the foot of her bed. Next to that door was the bathroom.

Jennifer laid in the hospital bed in which the head of the bed was positioned up in Semi-Fowlers at about forty-five degrees.

The thin cotton gown hung loosely from her shoulders, its pale fabric catching the light every time she shifted. It did little to conceal how out of place she looked there, too alert, too composed for someone who was supposed to be resting just after a major accident.

One sleeve of the gown had slipped just slightly over her left shoulder, revealing her collarbone, and she absently tugged it back into place as if the gesture were muscle memory rather than modesty.

Her eyeglasses rested at the bedside atop a folded chart, the lenses reflecting the muted glow of the room's lamp.

Her blond hair fell around her face in loose, unstyled waves, clearly brushed but not carefully arranged, as if grooming had been an afterthought. A faint crease lingered between her brows, the residue of concentration or worry, and her lips were pressed together in a line which suggested she was replaying events she hadn't yet found words for while engrossed in conversation on the hospital phone.

She looked like someone caught between states, patient and observer, vulnerable and formidable, still wrapped in the symbols of recovery, but already unmistakably moving beyond them.

Next to her a night table with the telephone she was currently using.

Jennifer held the receiver of the phone to the right side of her head as she twirled her finger in the coiled line.

"No, dad, that won't be necessary, I'm totally fine."

She paused.

"The doctors said they just want to run a few tests to make sure I'm okay..." Interrupted, she paused again.

"Yes, I was unconscious when I arrived, but I came to shortly after and they're keeping me for observation just to make sure nothing was missed."

She paused again to listen.

"I'm not exactly sure yet how it happened but I will figure it out."

She huffed as she was interrupted yet again and paused.

She then happened to see an older African American couple at the nurse's station and witnessed as someone pointed to the room she was in.

"Dad, dad, I'm good, I'm a doctor too," said Jennifer as she watched as the couple approached her room door.

The woman started to knock but Jennifer waved them in.

"Okay, okay dad, I'll see you then, but let me go, I have visitors and we can finish this conversation when you get here."

She held a finger up to the couple, signaling them to give her a minute. "I love you and please tell mom I love her too and not to worry, I'm okay. I'll see you soon!" She then hung up the phone.

"Tried to convince my dad he doesn't have to rush back from Philly but he insists!"

"That's how us father's are," started Henry as he extended his hand to Jennifer who accidentally shocked him causing him to pull back quickly.

"I'm sorry," she winced.

"Static electricity," suggested Henry as he looked around. "I'm Henry Linard, this is my wife, Patrice."

Patrice nodded in the affirmative. "Nice to meet you."

"He looks just like you," Jennifer spouted out quickly. Henry looked at her curiously.

"You're Daryl's parents, right?"

"Yes, yes we are," smiled Henry.

Jennifer smiled. "Well, how is he? I couldn't get any info, due to HIPPA I'm sure, but he did save my life, I was hoping to thank him."

Henry looked back at Patrice who started tearing up. He then turned back and faced Jennifer. "Well, that's just it," he started, "he's not too well, at least physically."

"What?" asked Jennifer.

"Not to get into all the specifics," but it seems that life as he knows it will never be the same."

Tears started to build up in the wells of Jennifer's eyes. "I don't understand," started Jennifer, "I thought maybe we both just got knocked unconscious and figured if I'm okay, he should have definitely been okay."

"What do you mean?" asked Patrice

"Well, I work with electricity and magnetism in my research and he was carrying me, which meant that I would have been the exit point for the electricity. If anything, I should have been the one who was hurt, not him. "

"You were both struck by lightning?" asked Henry.

"Yes," replied Jennifer, "he got me out of my car and actually started carrying me to his semi and on the way there…"

"At least we know how this happened," started Patrice.

"I am so, so, so sorry!" cried Jennifer.

"No baby," started Patrice, "that's just who our baby is, a heart of gold."

"We only came to meet you in order to see how you were," agreed Henry. "He'll be moved up to a room after he's transferred from recovery later today. When he wakes up, I'm sure he'll be glad to know you're okay."

Jennifer wiped the tears from her eyes. "Thank you," she said.

THREE

DR. ELENI KALLISTRATOS stood behind the observation glass with her hands folded loosely in front of her, watching the patient walk.

Eleni was striking in a way which never felt accidental.

She carried herself with effortless composure, tall and impeccably dressed, favoring tailored suits in muted tones, charcoal, navy, deep green, which emphasized authority rather than fashion. Her dark hair with blond highlights was worn neatly styled, rarely changing, as if consistency itself were a form of control.

Her eyes were sharp and calculating, rarely blinking when she listened. Whenever she smiled, it was measured, deliberate, and never fully reached her eyes.

Eleni spoke softly, but with such certainty that people leaned in without realizing they were being drawn closer.

She radiated intelligence, patience, and inevitability.

On the therapy floor, each step the patient took was measured. Deliberate. Perfect.

The man, mid-thirties, former construction worker according to the chart, crossed the length of the rehabilitation floor without hesitation. No limp. No visible strain.

The prosthetic responded instantly, translating intention into motion with a precision which bordered on elegant.

"Latency?" Eleni asked without looking away.

"Point-zero-two milliseconds," answered Dr. Nadia Feldman. "Well within tolerance."

Feldman had the look of someone who had learned to survive in rooms where she was never the most powerful voice.

Doctor Nadia Feldman was of average height, slender, with dark hair usually pulled back in a practical style which suggested long hours and little patience for vanity. She dressed conservatively, neutral blouses, slacks, low-heeled shoes, clothing chosen to blend into professional environments rather than dominate them.

Her face, though strikingly beautiful, bore the quiet tension of someone who thought faster than she spoke. Her eyes were observant, cautious, and often tired. When she spoke, it was precise, deliberate, as though every word had been weighed for consequence before leaving her mouth.

She looked like a woman who knew exactly where the lines were and what it would cost to cross them.

Eleni nodded. "Lower than yesterday."

Dr. Park shifted his weight while nodding affirmatively. "The spinal relay is adapting faster than we expected."

"It always does," Eleni replied. "The brain wants coherence. We're just giving it a cleaner path."

Behind her, Michael Rourke cleared his throat. "The board is ecstatic," he said. "Heritage is being mentioned alongside Johns Hopkins now. Donations are pouring in."

Eleni allowed herself a small smile.

"Visibility matters," she said. "Credibility even more."

The patient stopped walking and laughed softly, shaking his head as if he didn't quite believe himself.

"I don't feel the leg pain," he said. "But I know it's there."

Dr. Feldman made a note on her tablet.

"What he feels," Eleni said calmly, "is compliance and the blocking of pain receptors."

The others didn't respond. They didn't need to.

Beneath the patient's scalp, nestled against the motor cortex and threaded along the spinal column, the Helix interface chip pulsed faintly. It translated thought into movement. Movement into data. Data into response.

And response into access.

"Has the candidate been informed about the auxiliary protocols?" Dr. Haines asked.

"Yes," Feldman said. "Page twelve section A of the consent form. Whether he chose to read it or not is another question."

"Long as it's signed," muttered Dr. Haines.

Eleni turned from the glass at last.

"And the original injury?" she asked.

Dr. Park hesitated, just a fraction of a second.

"Degenerative disk disease," he said. "Amputation was... preventative, he of course didn't know that."

Eleni studied him.

"Good," she said. "We can't afford hesitation."

Rourke checked his watch and looked down at his tablet. "Another delivery arrives tomorrow. One right leg. One left arm. One spinal unit, all of which are measured for the next case."

"How many unnecessary?" Eleni asked.

Dr. Feldman barely looked up. "Hard to define 'necessary' anymore."

Eleni smiled again, this time without warmth.

"Exactly."

She turned back to the observation window as the patient took another step, stronger this time. Faster.

Connected.

"They think we're restoring what was lost," she said. "They never ask what we're adding."

None of them spoke.

Outside in the therapy gym, the patient paused, suddenly still, his expression briefly unfocused.

"Dr. Feldman," Eleni said quietly. "Did you feel that?"

"Yes," Feldman replied. "Signal spike. External handshake."

Eleni's smile widened.

"Good," she said. "The network is learning."

She clasped her hands behind her back.

"Soon," she continued, "they won't just move when they want to."

The patient resumed walking.

Eleni remained at the glass, watching the patient complete another pass across the floor before finally turning away.

"Who's next?" she asked.

Dr. Feldman tapped her tablet and scrolled. "Post-op recovery intake. Trauma case. Male. Late twenties."

Dr. Park leaned forward slightly. "That's the one from the interstate."

Eleni stopped walking.

"Which interstate?"

"Three seventy-six," Rourke said. "Storm. Electrical strike. Two victims. Both survived."

Eleni's eyes narrowed just a fraction. "Both survived? Are they both candidates?"

"The woman is a young doctor who also does work with electricity in vector kinematics and magnetism. Her father was a colleague of mine, We did longitudinal neurological studies on patients who were released during the Byberry Hospital shutdown in Philadelphia years ago. I excluded her from the project out of respect for her father," Feldman replied. "The candidate doesn't have any known neurological damage."

"It seems he absorbed most of the discharge," added Parks.

Eleni turned slowly and faced Feldman. "Next time you decide to exclude a candidate, run it by me first, no exceptions."

Feldman briefly felt a lump in the back of her throat.

"By any account," Haines interjected, "He shouldn't have lived."

"Neither of them should have," added Feldman, "but, no cardiac arrest, no spinal fracture, no neural degradation...Frankly, no permanent damage at all."

"Which is why we should use the other one too," added Eleni.

Silence filled the room.

Dr. Haines folded his arms. "We ran full imaging. MRI. CT. PET. Nothing abnormal."

"And yet," Eleni said calmly, "he's on your list."

"We altered the test results, life or death surgery needed." Rourke cleared his throat. "The parents signed as power of attorney. They were... cooperative."

"Cooperative," Eleni repeated. "Wonderful."

Dr. Park shifted uncomfortably. "Physically intact," he said. "Exceptionally so. Muscle density off the charts for his age. The prosthetic bonding will be smooth."

Eleni looked at Feldman. "Neurology?"

"No signs of impairment," Feldman admitted. "If anything, enhanced processing under stress, increased brainwave activity when under general."

Eleni smiled.

"Perfect," she said. "It will take a little more than normal to control him, but perfect."

Dr. Haines frowned. "The report states catastrophic limb trauma."

"States," Eleni echoed.

Dr. Park exhaled slowly. "We classified it as irreparable. Electrical burns with associated risks. Microfractures leading to long-term mobility failure."

"And the truth?" Eleni asked.

Dr. Park met her eyes. "None of that. He didn't need the amputations."

No one moved.

"He's strong," Feldman said quietly. "Stronger than the others. Whatever happened in that storm maybe did something to him."

Eleni turned back to the observation glass, though the rehabilitation floor now stood empty.

"What's his name?" she asked.

Feldman glanced at the screen. "Daryl Linard."

The name lingered.

"Age?" Eleni asked.

"Twenty-nine."

"Occupation?"

"Truck driver."

Eleni nodded slowly. "Grounded. Durable. Used to long hours. Isolation. Obedience to schedules."

Dr. Haines looked over at Dr. Park and swallowed. "You're thinking command compatibility?"

"I'm thinking resilience," Eleni replied. "Someone who is able to survive a lightning strike won't break easily."

Rourke adjusted his tie. "The parents were told the procedure would save his life."

"And they believed it?" Eleni asked.

"Yes."

"Good," she replied. "Belief is cleaner than coercion."

Feldman hesitated. "There's something else."

Eleni turned.

"The chip integration synced immediately," Feldman said. "No rejection. No latency curve. It was as if his nervous system... recognized it."

Eleni's smile returned, slower this time.

"Then he's not just another asset," she said. "He's a keystone."

Dr. Park stiffened. "What if he resists?"

Eleni stepped closer to the glass, her reflection faintly visible over the darkened room.

"Everyone resists," she said. "At first."

She turned back to them.

"That's why we don't control the limb," she continued. "We control the mind which moves the limb."

Silence again.

"When will he awake?" she asked.

"He's been awake," Feldman replied. "Already moved from PACU to one of the suites under the auspices of being a hero."

Eleni nodded. "Good. I want to be here after the limbs are attached and when he first stands."

FOUR

PATRICE LINARD WALKED quietly back to her son's bedside. She had been sitting next to him for hours, reading her book while Daryl slept.

Daryl's hospital suite was larger than expected, clearly designed for long-term as well as high-profile recovery.

The room was private, sound-dampened, with reinforced fixtures subtly embedded into the walls and floors.

Medical equipment such as in room EKG monitors stood next to an IV pump with the pole holding a patient-controlled analgesia or PCA pump, along with a time-controlled dynamap with neatly organized advanced monitoring systems quietly tracking vital signs and cardiac activity.

The bed itself was adjustable in multiple ways, with pressure redistribution air mattresses, foot board sequential flow devices, and even outlets to plug in electrical devices, more sophisticated than standard hospital accommodations.

Large windows overlooked the city, allowing natural light to flood the room during the day. At night, the glow from outside cast soft reflections across the polished surfaces.

It felt less like a patient's room and more like a hotel suite.

The sunlight was now streaming into the room, making Patrice realize it was time to draw the curtains close. As she got up and reached for the fabric, Daryl moaned, causing her to turn and face him.

"Leave it open momma, you know I love the light!" he said groggily.

Patrice smiled, happy to see her son awake and speaking. She quickly reopened the curtains and then moved to her son's side, kissing him on the forehead. "Oh baby, you gave us quite a scare," she said, her voice filled with relief.

Daryl opened his eyes and looked around, fully, taking in his surroundings. "Where's...dad?" he grunted as if uncomfortable, looking around the room.

Patrice's smile faltered for a moment before she answered.

"He had to go take care of Shadow; he'll be back. But there's something you need to know," she said, her tone becoming serious.

Daryl interrupted her as he adjusted himself a little and wiggled himself up a bit, "Left arm, right leg?" he asked, remembering the brief conversation he had prior to going fully under in the operating room. "I know, I know. For some strange reason, it hadn't quite hit me yet. I still feel like I have both the arm and the leg and they hurt like hell."

Patrice nodded, understanding the shock her son must be feeling. "That machine with the IV is supposed to give you Dilaudid on a schedule, but you can hit the button to get an extra dose when you need it or before they change your dressings," she explained, gesturing to the machine and the button.

Daryl looked at it and then back at his mom. "Yeah they explained it to me before I came up, but I was so tired from what they gave me, I fell back to sleep. I'll save it for a little later," he said, not wanting to rely on the medication.

Patrice again nodded as she adjusted her son's blanket, understanding her son's reluctance. "I met the young lady whose life you saved," she said, changing the subject.

Daryl's eyes widened a bit in surprise. "Really?" he asked. "How is she?"

Patrices' smile returned as she shared the good news. "Believe it or not, not a scratch on her."

Daryl let out a sigh of relief, grateful his actions had helped someone else.

Then he thought about it as he looked at his mother curiously. "You sure you met the right person? I am certain we were both struck."

Patrice shook her head in the affirmative. "She knew who me an' your father were before we even introduced ourselves, told us how you got her out of the car and were trying to carry her to your truck..."

"Wow, then this wasn't for nothing!"

"The doctor's will be up in a couple of days to talk with you about your prosthesis."

"Speaking of which," Daryl started as he grunted a little. He then quickly pushed the button to his PCA pump.

"Changed your mind?"

"Sure did!" he chuckled. "Robotic prosthetics and a suite? You don't think it's a little generous for a privately funded hospital?"

"We did," started Patrice, "but they consider you a hero and nothing but the best will do, according to the hospitalist!"

"Well, I'll do it, I want to try and maintain as much of my independence as possible."

"That's my baby!"

"Mama, my arm is itching a little a couple of inches above my I-V site. Do you mind?"

Patrice started scratching his arm. "Of course not!"

***

While in her room, Jennifer Harding put on her eyeglasses and picked up book to read and was briefly distracted by the lamp at her bedside flickering and she turned and looked at the lamp.

"Excuse me, Doctor Harding," interrupted Nurse Jessica.

Jennifer turned and faced the door as if caught off by surprise. "Huh?" she asked.

"I'm sorry," started the nurse, "your call bell went off and Colleen your care tech is a bit tied up so I came in to see if I could help you with anything?"

"Oh," started Jennifer, "no I'm good, and please, just call me Jennifer."

The nurse chuckled. "No problem let me just reach over you and turn off your call light!"

"It's on?" asked Jennifer with a surprised tone as she watched as the nurse depressed a button on her wall to deactivate the call light."

"Sometimes the button can be pushed accidentally," the nurse replied.

"Okay, thanks," replied Jennifer as she watched the nurse head out the room.

"No problem!" the nurse spouted back.

Jennifer looked back at her book as she opened it and she noticed the words looked a little blurry. She removed her glasses to clean them off but noticed she could now see the words more clearly. She put the glasses over her eyes and noticed that the words again looked blurry.

She removed them again.

Clear.

"What the fuck?" she whispered as she looked at her glasses. She then sat the glasses and the book down and slowly got out of the bed.

She went into the bathroom and switched on the light to examine her eyes, jumping back when she spied what looked to be little jolts of electricity roll across her eyes. "What the fuck?" she asked again.

"Excuse me young lady!" yelled a voice from behind the curtain. "Could you please not cuss like that in here? It's making me very uncomfortable."

"Sorry Misses Johnson!" spouted Jennifer as she looked from the bathroom door back into the mirror, while mouthing the words, *you're making me very uncomfortable*. She silently again mouthed the words, *What the fuck?*

She gazed down at her hands, flipping them from palms down to palms up and back again. Closing her door tightly, she cupped her hands together, bringing them closer and closer.

As her hands gained proximity to each other, sparks of electricity danced between her fingertips, causing her to silently gasp and mouth the words, *Oh my God!*

Gently pulling her fingers apart, the electricity dissipated. She repeated the motion, watching in wonder as the electricity crackled to life once more, causing a look of fear to spread across her face.

This time, it took a bit longer for the energy to fade.

Suddenly, a knock on the door broke her concentration and startled her. "Jennifer, are you alright?" asked Nurse Jessica through the door, her voice filled with concern. "Your call light went off again."

"I'm fine, Jessica," Jennifer reassured her with a lie. "I'm not sure why it keeps going off though."

"No problem," replied the nurse. "I'll have maintenance take a look at it for ya."

"Thanks, Jessica," Jennifer said gratefully as she reached over and pressed the call light button, saving the nurse from having to come in the bathroom. "I just pressed the button Jessica!"

"Okay, thank you!"

"Oh, and do you know when the neurologist will be in to see me?"

"I believe it's this afternoon," answered Jessica. "I think we're just waiting for your CT scans and x-rays to be resulted."

"Okay," Jennifer replied. "Thanks again."

"You're welcome," said the nurse.

Jennifer stared at herself in the mirror. "What is happening to me?"

FIVE

HENRY AND PATRICE Linard sat in the hospital cafeteria and looked around at the clean design of the facility.

She ordered a turkey club sandwich, and he had gotten a burger and fries, his go to order whenever he wasn't sure of what to order.

Henry ordered a Sprite soda to drink, and she had her usual cup of coffee, with three creams and four Splenda.

She took a sip of her coffee while glancing over at him.

"Don't say it Patrice," he said.

"You know he would have exercised better judgement and had avoided that accident if we hadn't told him to suppress that light, Crystal," she said anyway.

"Oh for God's sake, you remember the name he gave it?"

"Don't say you haven't?"

"I haven't!" he lied. And we don't know for sure that things would've turned out any differently."

"Sure we do," she started. "That gift of his was a Godsend and we asked him to suppress it all those years ago! Do you think he would have been a truck driver if we had allowed him to live to his full potential?"

"What's wrong with being a truck driver? It's a respectable job and he loves the open road!"

"Nothing's wrong with it," she agreed, "but he might have calculated something safe, or more lucrative..."

"I don't think so," he interrupted.

"Okay," she started, "maybe not! Maybe he would be still do-ing the same thing, but do you remember how much joy he had as a toddler with learning and reading?"

Henry put his half-eaten sandwich down and looked her in the eyes. "Yeah, I do," he said.

"I think we need to talk with him and remind him of Crystal so he can at least experience that joy again; she may be all he has now. He's gonna have to come back home with us, and maybe need skilled home nursing or therapy, this is going to push him right into depression. And I know that neither of us want that for our boy."

Henry Linard took another bite of his sandwich and started chewing as he stared at his wife. He then swallowed his food. "I think you're right," he agreed, "but I think we should wait until he at least gets home, give him time to get acclimated to his new situation before we throw this at him too."

Patrice thought about what he said. "Okay, we'll do it your way."

Henry then nodded his head toward her plate. "Now eat your sandwich, his wound care isn't gonna take all afternoon."

***

A soft knock sounded at the door.

"Come in," Jennifer said, still standing near the window op-posite the room, available as her roommate had been discharged and no one admitted to the bed yet.

The door opened and a woman stepped inside, tall and com-posed, her dark hair pulled neatly back. She wore a white coat, unwrinkled, with a tablet tucked under her arm.

"Jennifer Harding?" the woman asked.

"Yes," Jennifer replied.

"I'm Dr. Feldman," she said. "Neurology."

Jennifer nodded. "Hi."

Dr. Feldman closed the door behind her and glanced briefly around the room, taking in the equipment, the lamp, the bed, the wall outlets. Nothing lingered long enough to feel obvious.

"How are you feeling?" Feldman asked.

"Fine," Jennifer answered quickly. "Just sore." She then paused. "You look familiar, have we met?"

Not since you were five, she thought. "I don't think so," she lied.

"I get that a lot," Feldman said. "Any headaches? Dizziness? Confusion?"

Jennifer shook her head. "No."

Dr. Feldman smiled faintly. "Good. I just need to run through a few simple checks. It won't take long."

She set the tablet down and pulled a small penlight out of her breast pocket.

"Follow the light with your eyes," she said.

Jennifer did as instructed. Left. Right. Up. Down.

Dr. Feldman watched closely, her expression neutral.

"Any trouble focusing?" she asked.

"Nah," Jennifer said, then hesitated. "I mean... no."

Dr. Feldman paused for just a moment, then continued.

"Hold your arms out for me."

Jennifer extended them.

Dr. Feldman pressed gently against her palms. "Resist," she said as she pressed down on her palms.

Jennifer did.

"Good," Feldman murmured as she stopped. "Very good."

She moved to Jennifer's side, tapping lightly along her left forearm, and then her shoulder.

"Do you feel that?"
"Yes."

Feldman repeated tapping on the right side.

"Both sides the same?"

"Yes."

Dr. Feldman stepped back and made a note on her tablet.

"Can you count backward from one hundred by sevens?"

Jennifer blinked. "Uh...okay. One hundred. Ninety-three. Eighty-six. Seventy-nine..."

Feldman kept typing on the tablet. "Keep going."

"Seventy-two. Sixty-five. Fifty-eight."

Dr. Feldman nodded. "That's fine."

She clicked off the penlight and slipped it back into her pocket.

"No signs of neurological deficit," she said calmly. "Your scans look clean. Reflexes are normal. Cognition intact."

Jennifer let out a breath she hadn't realized she was holding. "So... I'm good?" she asked.

Dr. Feldman met her eyes. "Yes. You're very lucky."

Jennifer smiled weakly. "That's what everyone keeps saying."

Dr. Feldman studied her for a moment longer, then turned toward the door.

"The hospitalist will likely clear you for discharge in the next day or so," she said. "Once the rest of your tests come back."

"Okay," Jennifer replied. "Thank you, Doctor."

Dr. Feldman paused with her hand on the door. *Wow, she is extremely lucky*, she thought.

"One more thing," she said, turning back. "If you notice anything unusual, vision changes, numbness or tingling in your extremities, or any other odd sensations, you should let someone know."

Jennifer nodded. "I will."

Dr. Feldman gave her a final, unreadable look.

"Get some rest," she said.

The door closed softly behind her.

Jennifer stood there for a moment, listening to the hum of the room. She glanced at the lamp by her bed.

It stayed steady.

She flexed her fingers slowly, carefully, as if afraid of what might happen if she didn't.

Nothing did.

Still, she didn't relax.

SIX

DARYL LAID STILL in his hospital bed as the wound nurse finished wrapping the bandage on his left upper limb.

"Everything looks good Mr. Linard," she said as she applied
a final piece of tape on the top which had the date and time written in black marker. "The surgeons will be in sometime today to
discuss your prosthetics with you."

Daryl smiled. "Oh the joy of getting fake limbs."

"Oh I think you'll appreciate these, I'll see you tomorrow
Mister Linard," the nurse said smilingly. As she turned and
headed out the door, Jennifer had just knocked and was making
her way in holding a small plastic bag as well as a vase with
flowers.

Jennifer nodded and smiled at the nurse who reciprocated
as they passed each other.

As she got closer to Daryl, she could tell from the impression
that his right leg was amputated pretty high above the knee.

The left arm was exposed so she could see he only had a
stump on that side neatly dressed and wrapped.

Her smile started to fade.

"Hey," started Daryl gleefully, "are those gift shop flowers
for me?"

"Nothing but the best for my hero!" she said smilingly as she
sat the vase on his nightstand. She then hugged him.

"My mom was right," he started, "you look incredibly well!"

"Good genes I suppose!" she spouted unsure of what to say,
then she started tearing up. "I am so, so very sorry this happened to you!"

"Daryl looked at his lap and then looked back up at her. "Really Jennifer, it's okay!"

"How are you able to stay this positive after," she paused and started sobbing again.

"Something deep down inside of me tells me over and over again that everything'll be okay," started Daryl, "and I need to believe that that's true!"

She smiled. "You are such an amazing guy!"

"When I get my prosthetics, who knows? I may be the next bionic man?" he joked. "They are doing amazing things with prosthetics these days!"

She laughed. "I'll be your trusty assistant!"

Daryl grew a puzzled look on his face. "I don't remember the Bionic Man ever having an assistant!"

"Well, it would please me to be the first!"

They both laughed.

"I better go, my father is waiting downstairs for me," she said as she looked at the vase of flowers, "but I put my phone number inside the card there. If you ever need anything and I can help you, please let me know!"

"Thank you," he said smilingly. "And thank you for stopping to see me Jennifer."

"It's the least I could do," she said as she hugged him again. She then left out of the room.

Daryl reached over to the vase with his right hand while wincing in discomfort and retrieved the card from the vase, opening it.

To My Hero with Love,
Jennifer
717-555-1734

The door had barely closed behind Jennifer when Daryl heard familiar voices in the hallway.

"Daryl?" his mother called softly.

"Mom?" he replied, quickly sliding the card back into the vase.

Henry and Patrice Linard entered the room together, his father carrying a folded jacket over his arm, his mother already halfway to her son's bedside.

She leaned down carefully and kissed him on the cheek.

"There you are," she said, her voice catching. "You look better than you did yesterday."

Daryl smiled. "That's because the pain meds are doing their job."

Henry chuckled faintly but his eyes didn't leave his son. He took in the bandages, the machines, the empty space where limbs should have been. His jaw tightened.

"We just missed the young woman," Henry said. "The one you helped."

"Jennifer," Daryl replied. "She's doing great."

"That's good," his mother said. "That's very good."

There was a knock at the door.

Henry turned around just as the door fully opened, revealing three doctors standing together.

One of them Daryl recognized immediately.

"Mr. and Mrs. Linard?" asked Dr. Feldman.

"Yes," Henry replied, stepping aside. "Please."

Dr. Feldman soon entered first, followed by two orthopedic surgeons, Dr. Victor Haines and Dr. Leonard Park. Haines was taller and broad-shouldered, his salt-and-pepper hair cropped neatly and short.

Park was kind looking, thinner, meticulous, looking preppy in his wardrobe. His dark hair combed neatly and his glasses were perched low on his nose.

"Daryl," Feldman said warmly. "How are you feeling?"

"Like a science experiment," he replied lightly.

Haines smiled. "That's actually not far off."

They all took positions around the bed. Feldman stood closest to Daryl's head. Haines near his right side. Park at the foot of the bed.

"We wanted to talk with you and your parents together," Feldman began, "about your prosthetics."

Daryl glanced at his parents. His mother nodded gently.

"These aren't conventional prosthetics," Haines continued. "They're fully robotic. Adaptive. Integrated."

Parks picked up. "They interface directly with your nervous system, both the spinal cord and the motor cortex of your brain."

Daryl frowned. "You mean... wired in?"

"In a manner of speaking," Feldman said calmly. "You already have the neural interface implanted, as discussed, I placed it myself after your amputations."

Daryl's eyes widened. "The chip?"

"Yes," Feldman replied. "It integrates with your brain and spinal cord and will allow the prosthetics to communicate with your brain as if they were natural limbs."

Henry stepped forward. "Wait, he already has something in his head?"

"It was in the clause you signed as P-O-A, necessary to be done," Feldman said smoothly. "Given the trauma, it was the safest way to ensure compatibility when he was ready for the application of the prosthetics."

Daryl swallowed. "I'm not gonna lie... having body parts that talk back to my brain freaks me out a little."

"There is always two-way communication occurring between the central nervous system and the peripheral nervous system," Feldman said. "But the chip doesn't control you. It interprets electrical signals your brain already produces and translates them into movement."

Haines leaned in. "Think of it like a translator. Your brain speaks one language. The prosthetics speak another. The chip just makes sure they understand each other."

Daryl let out a slow breath. "So it's not... thinking for me?"

"No," Feldman said without hesitation. "It only responds when you do."

His mother reached for his hand. "If this helps you walk again..."

"It will," Haines said confidently. "You'll actually be able to do many of the same things you did prior to the accident, but, for the procedure, having it sooner is better than later."

Daryl looked up. "Sooner?"

"The longer we wait," Parks explained, "the more your body adapts to the loss. Scar tissue forms. Neural pathways weaken; rejection of the system becomes a strong possibility. If we proceed now, the cohesiveness between your body and the prosthetics will be significantly stronger."

"Healing time?" Henry asked.

"Much, much faster than without our chip and prosthetics," Haines said. "Cleaner."

Feldman nodded in agreement with Haines. "You're young. You're healthy. Your physiology is ideal. Waiting would only work against you."

Daryl stared at the ceiling for a moment, processing.

"So," he said finally, "you're saying if I do this now... I have a better shot at getting my life back."

"Yes," Feldman said simply.

He looked at his parents.

His mother's eyes were already wet.

His father nodded once.

"Alright," Daryl said. "Let's do it."

Feldman smiled. "Good decision."

None of the surgeons mentioned how ideal Daryl truly was.

SEVEN

THE OPERATING ROOM was colder than Daryl expected.

Bright lights hovered overhead, bleaching the color from everything beneath them. The hum of machines filled the air, steady and mechanical, broken only by the occasional beep from the monitors beside him.

Dr. Feldman stood near his head, partially obscured by her mask.

"Daryl," she said calmly, "we're going to begin shortly."

He nodded, trying to ignore the tightness in his chest.

Dr. Victor Haines stood on his left side, already scrubbed in, reviewing images displayed on a large monitor, spinal cross-sections, neural pathways highlighted in soft blues and greens.

Dr. Leonard Park moved with practiced ease near the lower end of the table, double checking many of the instruments, confirming measurements, his voice low and confident as he spoke with the surgical staff.

Park looked up. "Final verification complete," Park said. "Haines?"

"Confirmed," Haines replied. "Interface points are clean."

Daryl shifted his eyes toward Feldman. "This thing in my head... it's already on, right?"

Feldman lowered. Her head and leaned closer so only he could hear her. "It is passive right now. It's listening, not speaking."

She didn't comfort him as much as she probably intended.

The anesthesiologist stepped forward and looked at Daryl. "You'll feel a little heaviness in your chest," he said. "That's normal."

Daryl took one last breath, staring at the ceiling tiles.

"See you on the other side," Park said, almost casually.

The room softened.

The lights blurred.

And then—

Nothing.

***

Jennifer sat at the small kitchen table, a mug of untouched tea cooling between her hands.

Her father stood at the counter, jacket draped over the back of a chair, reading glasses perched low on his nose as he flipped through the discharge paperwork she'd brought home. He hadn't said much since he arrived, which worried her more than if he had.

"You were lucky," Dr. Michael Harding said finally, not looking up.

Dr. Michael Harding had aged the way men do when their lives had been shaped more by responsibility than by indulgence.

His hair, once dark and neatly kept, had thinned and turned a dignified silver at the temples, receding just enough to expose the passing of his years without diminishing his presence. What remained was kept short and practical, the habit of a man who never cared much for vanity.

His face bore the quiet lines of experience, fine creases around the eyes from years of focus and concern, deeper ones at the corners of his mouth from conversations which had rarely ended lightly.

There was no softness to him, but neither was there hardness. Instead, he carried the composed gravity of someone who had spent decades making decisions which mattered, often without the luxury of certainty.

His posture remained straight, though no longer effortless. He moved with deliberate economy, conserving energy rather than wasting it, as if each motion had been evaluated and approved before being made.

When he stood still, there was a sense that he was listening, to people, to rooms, to silence.

His eyes were unchanged.

Still sharp. Still observant. Still capable of cutting through pretense with a single look.

They held the kind of intelligence which didn't rush to speak, paired with a caution born from having once been younger and more confident.

If there was weariness in them now, it came not from doubt, but from knowing how easily good intentions could be bent into something else.

Harding dressed simply, pressed slacks, a button-down shirt, sometimes a blazer he rarely bothered to button. No jewelry. No unnecessary adornments. Even out of the hospital, he looked like a physician, the role having long since ceased to be something he *did* and become something he *was*.

When he spoke, his voice was lower than it used to be, steadier, each word chosen with care. He never wasted time raising his voice. He learned people listened more closely when he didn't.

Above all, Dr. Harding carried the unmistakable presence of a man who had seen too much to be naïve, but not enough to become cruel.

A man who remembered every patient.

A man who understood, perhaps better than most, that some lives change in an instant, and others do so over time.

Jennifer exhaled. "That's what everyone keeps telling me."

Harding turned a page. "Your magnetic, antigravitational electricity generator overheating during a live demonstration," he said. "Followed by a complete power outage?"

She nodded. "The stabilizers failed. I shut it down before it collapsed, but the field spiked. Fried half the components."

"What were you going to use it for?"

"It was a prototype for a plan to create self-reproducing energy for hover cars."

"Science fiction?" he scoffed. "And then," he continued, eyes narrowing slightly, "you drive straight into a lightning storm."

Jennifer gave a humorless smile. "Arizona timing."

"You're in Pittsburgh now!"

Her shoulders raised. "Dad, I've been reviewing my notes from the prototype and indicated risks, and I believe I somehow pulled the electricity during that storm toward me and Daryl."

"Dear God," he started, "are you saying that because you feel responsible for what happened to that young man who saved you?"

"Never mind," she sighed in frustration.

"Well, it wasn't your fault." Harding sat the papers down and looked at her fully now.

"Jennifer," he said gently, "you understand why I may be concerned?"

She met his gaze. "Yes...and no, dad, I wasn't doing anything reckless. I was very careful; I wouldn't risk my life or my medical license."

"I reviewed your notes too when I first heard what happened. That device," he said, tapping the folder in front of him as he looked down and then up at her again, "shouldn't have failed the way it did."

"I know," she replied quietly. "It was stable. I triple-checked the math."

Harding leaned back against the counter, arms folded. "And then there's this."

He picked up another page.

"Neurology consult," he read. "Dr. Nadia Feldman."

Jennifer's stomach tightened.

"That's the neurologist," she said. "She cleared me neurologically prior to my discharge."

Harding's expression shifted, subtle, but unmistakable.

"Feldman," he repeated.

"You know her?" Jennifer asked.

Harding hesitated just long enough for her to notice.

"I worked with her years ago," he said carefully. "Early in her career, during the Byberry incident. Brilliant. Ambitious. Very interested in neural interfaces."

Jennifer frowned. "She acted strange when I asked if we'd met before."

Harding studied her face. "Did she say anything unusual?"

"No," Jennifer replied. "That's what was weird. It felt like she was choosing every word."

Harding nodded slowly, then gathered the papers and slid them back into their folder. "She was at the house many times when you were a child, four or five I think, I'm sure your brother and sister would remember."

"They should they're almost two decades older than me," She huffed. "I thought she looked familiar!"

"Just...be careful," he said. "Between the accident, the storm, and the stress, your nervous system's been through a lot."

Jennifer smiled faintly. "You don't know the half, and stop sounding like my doctor."

Harding returned the smile, tired but affectionate. "In my mind, I am your doctor. I just happen to be your father too."

He leaned in and kissed her forehead. "Get some rest. Call me if anything feels...off."

"I will," she promised and lied.

Harding paused at the door, glanced back once more, then left.

Jennifer quickly locked the door behind him.

She checked it twice.

The house was quiet, the kind of quiet which made every small sound feel amplified. She moved her purse down carefully, as if it might react badly to sudden movement, then crossed the room and pulled the blinds closed.

The sky outside had already dimmed to a bruised orange.

She stood in the center of the room and took a slow breath.

"Okay," she whispered. "Okay."

She held her hands out in front of her, palms facing each other, keeping them farther apart than she had in the hospital. Her heart thudded loudly in her chest.

Nothing happened.

She frowned.

Slowly, deliberately, she brought her hands closer.

At first there was only the faintest sensation, like static before a storm. Then she saw it.

A thin, blue-white thread jumped between her fingertips.

Jennifer sucked in a sharp breath and pulled her hands apart.

The energy snapped away instantly.

She stared at her fingers, flexing them, checking for burns. There were none.

"Again," she said softly.

This time she brought her hands together more confidently.

The air between them shimmered.

Electricity danced in erratic arcs, brighter now, louder. She could feel it, not pain, not heat, but awareness. As if something inside her had finally been given permission to speak.

Her breathing quickened.

"Stop," she told herself.

The energy lingered for a moment longer than before, then faded reluctantly.

Jennifer stepped back, her legs suddenly unsteady. She grabbed the back of a chair to steady herself, laughing quietly under her breath.

"This isn't possible," she said.

She glanced toward the light switch.

After a brief hesitation, she reached out without touching it.

The lamp flicked on.

Jennifer froze.

She withdrew her hand slowly. The light stayed on.

A chill ran through her.

She turned away from the lamp and sat down heavily, pressing her palms flat against her thighs.

"Okay," she whispered again, but this time it sounded less like reassurance and more like warning.

She closed her eyes.

And that was when the floor stopped feeling solid.

Jennifer's eyes snapped open.

Her feet weren't touching the ground.

Only an inch at first, but unmistakable.

She gasped and flailed instinctively, bumping lightly into the kitchen counter as gravity seemed to remember her again and set her down with a soft thud.

She stood there, heart racing, staring at the spot where her feet had been.

"No," she whispered.

Slowly, carefully, she tried again, not jumping, not pushing, just *letting go*.

The air lifted her.

She rose a foot, then two, drifting upward until her shoulder brushed the underside of the cabinet.

Jennifer pressed her palm against it, grounding herself, and slowly sank back down.

She stood there shaking, hands clenched at her sides.

Outside, thunder rumbled faintly in the distance.

Jennifer looked up toward the ceiling, her breath shallow.
Something had changed.
And it wasn't done changing yet.

EIGHT

THE CONFERENCE ROOM overlooked the hospital's east wing.

Glass walls. Polished table. No windows that opened.

Being the largest financier of the hospital, Eleni Kallistratos always sat at the head of the table, composed, elegant, fingers steepled lightly in front of her.

The medical team took their seats around her, Feldman, Haines, Park, and finally, the hospital administrator Michael Rourke, whose expression was already sour.

Rourke exhaled sharply. "Do you have any idea what this latest procedure cost us?"

Eleni didn't look at him immediately.

"Not just the procedure, but the top notch care we're providing for this candidate. The hospital absorbs millions in uncompensated care," he continued. "Equipment, staff hours, liability..."

"And in return," Eleni interrupted calmly, "your pockets personally get those losses back, your institution remains ranked among the most advanced trauma centers in the country."

Rourke frowned. "That doesn't balance the books."

Eleni turned to him then, her gaze cool and precise.

"You can take some of that money lining your coat pockets and donate it anonymously back to the hospital if you're feeling conflicted."

The room went quiet.

"This Daryl Linard, who is young, physically exceptional, before his loss of limbs that is, and neurologically adaptable," Eleni continued. "Represents a return on investment far beyond reimbursement models previously predicted which will help put this hospital well into black."

Rourke shifted in his seat. "You're talking about a patient."

"I'm talking about an asset," Eleni replied without raising her voice.

Dr. Park glanced toward Feldman, who said nothing.

Haines cleared his throat. "Integration is progressing as expected."

"Good," Eleni said. "Then we move forward."

She tapped her tablet, projecting an image onto the screen.

A figure appeared fully dressed in fatigues, sleek, mask covering the lower half of his face. The uniform was matte black with minimal markings. The face covering seamless, reflective, unreadable.

"Uniform and mask design," Eleni said. "No insignia. No identifiers. Agents remain anonymous to each other and to the public."

Rourke frowned again. "Agents?"

"Voluntolds really," Eleni smiled devilishly. "Participants or Intelligent Computerized Enforcement agents."

Feldman studied the image. "And control parameters?"

"Remain invisible," Eleni said. "The connection must never be traced back here or to Helix."

She rose from her chair.

"When people ask how this hospital stays ahead," she said, "you will tell them we invest in the future."

She paused at the door.

"And the future," she added, "is most definitely obedient."

NINE

DARYL AWOKE TO the sound of squeaky wheels.
At first he thought he was dreaming, the low hum and soft rattle folding into the edge of sleep.

Then the sound grew clearer, rubber against tile, metal clicking softly, and then he opened his eyes.

A wheelchair sat at the foot of his bed.

For a moment, panic flared in his chest. Then he realized something else.

He didn't hurt.

Not the dull, throbbing pain he'd been bracing for. Not the sharp reminders his body should have been screaming at him. There was pressure, yes. Awareness, yes. But pain, no.

"Daryl?" his mother asked softly.
He turned his head.

Both of his parents were there, standing close, watching him as if he might vanish if they blinked.

"I think..." he started, then stopped.

Slowly and cautiously, Daryl shifted his weight and pushed himself upright.
His parents froze, surprised that his new metallic left arm was working as well as it had.

Daryl just woke up and had not yet been to therapy.

He swung his legs over the side of the bed and sat there, perfectly balanced. His new robotic right leg looked like the silver twin to his left leg.

The same went for his arms, his left robotic arm seemed to match his right arm almost identically except for being silver.

The metallic musculature flexed as if skin, yet it was obviously not skin.

"Oh my God," Patrice whispered.
Daryl looked down.

His legs, both legs, were there. Sleek, unmoving but present, solid. And he could feel both of them. His feet clearly placed firmly on the floor.

Still no pain.

"Daryl," his father said, voice tight, "don't…"

"I'm okay," Daryl interrupted, surprised by how steady he sounded.

He stood.

Not shakily. Not with effort. He stood as if he had done it a thousand times before.

Then he raised his new left hand and marveled at how well his arm and hand moved with his thoughts as if they truly were one.

He wiggled the fingers on his left hand.

He then looked down and wiggled his toes on his right foot.

Patrice covered her mouth.

His father reached out, instinctively, but Daryl didn't wobble.

He looked down at himself, flexed his fingers, rolled his shoulders.

"This is…" He laughed softly. "This is insane."

He then started walking around the room laughing.

Henry made a face of disgust. "Son your ass is all hangin' out!" He reached into a nearby closet and grabbed some boxer briefs and threw them at Daryl.

Daryl caught them with his left hand and then laughed. "Hey…hey!" he exclaimed. He then slipped the briefs on as his mother turned the other way.

A knock.

Then the door opened.

"Good morning, Mr. Linard," the physical therapist said brightly. "I see you're ready for your first post-op therapy session?"

Daryl glanced back at his parents, still standing there in stunned silence.

"Guess so," he said.

She positioned the chair behind them and locked the brakes.

He sat down easily.

The therapist then unlocked the brakes.

As they began to wheel him out, Patrice stepped forward.

"We'll come with him," she said.

The therapist smiled apologetically. "I'm sorry, family won't be able to attend this session."

"What?" Henry asked. "Why not?"

"Protocol," she replied. "There will be other patients in the area, and we have to maintain HIPPA. You can wait here; this won't take long."

Daryl frowned. "You sure they can't come?"

"Very sure," she said, already turning the chair.

His parents exchanged a look and Daryl shrugged while mouthing the word, *protocol*!

***

The therapy gym was larger than he expected. He looked around at it and compared to his high school gym. It had a wide-open floor but the size of the area was where the similarities, ceased.

Different than his high school gym though, there were rein-forced bars along the walls. Sensors were embedded in the ceiling and floor. A row of observation glass on one side which reflected back at the patients like a long mirror.

Dr. Park stood by, waiting as the therapist rolled the chair to the edge of the parallel bars.

"Hey doc," how come I don't feel any pain?" asked Daryl.

Dr. Park smiled. "Because the chip along with the prosthetics have suppressed your pain receptors. We can turn them on if you want?"

"Naw, naw, " started Daryl. "I'm good"!

"Alright," Park said cheerfully. "Let's see what you can do."

They didn't start slow.

"Stand," Park said.

Daryl stood up from the chair.

"Walk."

He walked.

"Turn."

Daryl effortlessly turned around.

"Start walking again."

Daryl started walking back towards the therapist.

"Stop."

Daryl immediately stopped walking.

"Now," started Park as he started pointing around the room, "you see the parallel lines going around the room?"

"I see them," said Daryl.

"I want you to walk around the room, inside that track, normal pace."

Daryl walked over to the track and started following it around the room. He maintained his stride for about five minutes.

"Accelerate."

Daryl easily complied, each command he answered instantly, his body responding with an ease which made him smile and then laugh.

"You okay?" Park asked.

"I feel... great," Daryl said honestly as he kept walking.

Dr. Feldman watched quietly while smiling from the edge of the room, tablet in hand.

"Now run!"

"Daryl started running on command with ease.

"Jump," Park said.

Daryl hesitated. Then he jumped.

Higher than he meant to, over six feet up.

He landed perfectly and continued running.

His heart raced. "Did you see that?"

"Yes," Park said, eyes bright. "Again."

Daryl jumped again, this time, over eight feet up. When he landed, he stopped running.

"How come I don't feel the landing on my left leg? The regular one!"

The prosthetics are smart myelion neurotitanium,"started Park. "Which is a fancy way of saying the smart metal is paying attention to the messages carried along your nerves, so it knows it has to take most of the impact of your landing. Your touchdown occurs in a fraction of a second, so you barely notice your left foot touch down after the right one."

Daryl smiled again and then laughed as he started running around the track again followed by a series of jumps. "Whoo Hoo!"

Parks laughed.

They pushed him harder. Faster.

Balance tests.

He passed.

Resistance tests.

He passed

Sudden directional changes.

Passed.

Strength measurements which made Park's eyebrows lift.

Passed.

Behind the glass, unseen, Eleni Kallistratos stood with her arms folded. Smiling.

"Continue," she said softly into her headset.

Park, looking in the direction of the two-way mirror, blinked, surprised, but nodded.

They escalated.

Daryl ran until his lungs burned, but his body never faltered. Something in particular was different about his body in contrast with the other candidates, and Eleni knew it even if Daryl didn't.

He lifted weights three times his own and realized he could do so effortlessly.

"This doesn't make sense," he muttered.

"It does, it makes perfect sense," Eleni said quietly, though he couldn't hear her.

When it was finally over, Daryl stood in the center of the room, breathing hard, grinning like a kid who had just discovered he could fly.

"I passed, right?" he asked.

Park laughed. "You shattered every benchmark we had, and then some."

Behind the glass, Eleni smiled.

TEN

BY THE END of the week, Daryl had been discharged from the hospital but had opted to stay at his parents' home in the event he needed them.

Daryl laid quietly in his old bed at his parents' home and marveled at his level of comfort after all he had been through. He stared at his left hand and marveled at it.

Shadow, his father's Labrador, slept soundly at the foot of his bed.

Within the hour, he fell sound asleep.

Shadow soon popped his head up and started growling.

Everyone was asleep until Daryl's eyes opened and he sat up on the side of his bed. His actions robot-like. He quickly got up and got dressed. He then put his sneakers on, grabbed a skully and placed it on his head.

Shadow started barking incessantly.

"SHADOW!" called Henry from his own room as the dog continued barking.

Shadow continued to bark as Daryl moved robot like towards the door.

Hearing the commotion Henry came out of his room just in time to see Daryl walking out the front door of the house and Shadow barking as he left out the door.

"DARYL!" Henry called, but the door closed.

His call to his son went unheard.

Daryl started running with the swiftness of an athlete.

It happened just hours after his release from the hospital.

Eleni, anxious to exploit him.

He moved with speed which wasn't human, precision that didn't feel like choice.

The address, sent to the chip in his head, and now the chip controlling him and telling him to go and retrieve someone she wanted.

The air was cold and crisp, but he didn't feel it.

His strides caught the glares of passers-by, but he didn't care.

He soon found the house he was looking for and ran up to the door and stopped.

He then knocked on the door as if he had an urgent matter to discuss.

The light to the living room window came on.

Then the porch light illuminated.

The security chain rattled.

Then the door lock clicked.

Jennifer opened the door and looked from side to side. "Daryl? Is everything okay? How'd you get my..."

His sudden grabbing of her neck cut her words off as he carried her into the house while lifting her up higher with one hand.

His uploaded objective: *bring her to Helix alive, break at least one arm and one leg, but bring her back alive!*

She gasped and then suddenly electricity crackled around her body, shocking him and causing him to lose his grip.

He dropped her.

She breathed in heavily.

He surveyed the electrical burns on his right hand.

"Daryl," she gasped. "Why are you doing this? Wait...how are you even walking?"

He came at her again and swung his left arm into her. She went flying back across the living room and crashed into a wall."

She fell to the floor, wiped the blood off the side of her face, and looked at him angrily.

That can't be him, she thought, *or someone is controlling him. Either way I gotta stop him, or he will kill me!*

She screamed as she aimed both hands out in front of herself towards him and fired electricity straight at him.

The fight was brutal, chaotic, him striking without knowing he was, her defending herself on instinct.

He tried to move forward.

"Daryl, STOP!" she shouted.

He couldn't.

When she finally screamed and unleashed everything inside her, the electricity didn't just hit him, it found something.

His metallic limbs appeared to vibrate.

He collapsed, falling backwards.

She rushed to his side.

His left arm and right leg both buzzed with electricity as the torn and burned clothing revealed to her metal limbs.

"What the..."

"Ja...Jennifer?" Daryl asked. "What's ga...going on?" He asked, the pain firing all over his body.

"I was just going to ask you the same thing."

"One minute, I was at my parents' house falling asleep, and the next thing I know, I wake up here with you standing over me."

"Daryl, you're at my house!"

Daryl looked around with confusion on his face. "If someone sent me here to kill you..."

"Then neither of us are safe here."

"Can you take me to my parents' house? We will be safe there until we can figure out what's going on?"

Jennifer nodded in agreement. "Can you stand?"

"I think so, but I need a little help."

***

The Helix Systems building dominated its surroundings with deliberate intimidation.

The exterior was composed of dark glass, steel, and angular architecture which reflected the sky while concealing the interior completely. The structure had no unnecessary ornamentation, every line purposeful, every angle sharp.

Security was visible but understated: controlled access points, surveillance embedded seamlessly into the design. At night, the building glowed faintly from within, like a machine which never fully powered down.

It looked less like a corporate headquarters, and more like a fortress.

Inside Helix Systems, the atmosphere was sterile and hyper-efficient.

The interior was dominated by cool lighting, glass walls, and smooth metallic surfaces. Offices were open but segmented, allowing visibility without intimacy. Data screens glowed constantly, feeding real-time information into the space like a living organism.

Sound was minimal. Conversations were quiet. Footsteps echoed faintly.

Everything about the interior suggested precision, hierarchy, and control.

The control room was dark except for the wall of monitors.

Data scrolled in steady columns of light, heart rate, neural activity, spinal relay output, each metric updating in real time until, suddenly, it didn't.

The Helix Systems technician froze.

"Dr. Kallistratos," he said quietly.

Eleni looked up from her tablet. "What is it?"

The technician swallowed and gestured to the central display. "We've lost signal from Asset Linard."

Eleni didn't move.

"Define lost," she said.

"The control chip just went offline," the tech replied. "No telemetry. No received up-link. No fail-over."

He hesitated before adding, "Vitals dropped to zero."

Silence settled over the room.

Eleni set her tablet down slowly and walked toward the screen.

The data stream remained frozen, a flat line where motion had been moments before.

"Run it again," she said.

The technician complied, pulling up the recorded timeline.

"This is him leaving the residence," he explained, pointing as a map populated the screen. "Elevated heart rate, increased motor output. No hesitation."

The playback continued.

"This is him running," the tech said. "Top speed, well beyond baseline projections."

The map jumped.

"And here, this is Jennifer Harding's address."

On the screen, the vitals spiked violently.

His heart rate surged. Neural activity flared in chaotic waves. Power output from the spinal interface jumped erratically, climbing far past safe thresholds.

"This," the technician said softly, "looks like a fight."

The data became jagged, unstable, then abruptly stopped.

"And this," he finished, "is where everything goes dark."

Eleni stared at the screen for a long moment.

"Dead," the young but intelligent technician said. "At least according to the system."

Eleni reached out and rewound the feed herself, slower this time. She studied the neural spikes, the irregular patterns, the sudden surges many of which didn't align with Helix's control architecture.

She smiled.

"Run a comparative overlay," she said. "Cross-reference with data sets in which the chips were fried.

The technician frowned but complied.

As the two data sets overlapped, similarities began to appear, brief but undeniable.

Electrical surges.

Unmapped interference.

Signals which didn't originate from Daryl at all.

Eleni's smile widened.

"So," she murmured, "she is special too."

The technician looked at her. "Ma'am?"

"She disrupted the control field," Eleni said calmly. "She somehow presented with an energy output which neutralized the chip."

She folded her arms. "I knew there was something special about her, now I just need to learn what and how to best exploit her."

The technician hesitated. "Wouldn't a neutralized chip cause him to be incapacitated as well?"

"His prosthetics would be useless, dead weight but it wouldn't necessarily cause him to die unless something external exploded the chip."

"What are your orders?"

Eleni didn't hesitate at all.

"Dispatch two Intelligent Computerized Enforcement agents from that vicinity," she said. "Standard retrieval protocol. Bring Linard's body to me and bring Jennifer Harding in, alive!"

"Yes, ma'am."

ELEVEN

DARYL LAID ON the couch, shaking, his limbs jerking subtly as if struggling to obey him.

"I don't know why I attacked you," he said hoarsely. "Everything hurts!"

Jennifer watched him closely. "Something made you attack me and I will figure it out."

His parents looked between them, terrified.

That was when Henry spoke.

"Daryl, there's something we need to tell you," He said.

They spoke of the blue light Daryl had manifested as a child and he said, "you told us we only had to say one word in order to unlock your memories. Crystal."

"Crystal?" Daryl asked. His eyes soon closed and started to flutter for several minutes.

He then suddenly went still.

Too still.

"What'd you do?" asked Jennifer.

"HANK!" screamed Patrice

Henry grew nervous. "Give him a minute now, it's been over twenty-four years!"

Inside of his body, the blue light zipped up and down his DNA strands and altering his entire structure.

Then—

He stood all the way up.

"Analysis complete," he said flatly. "Preparing body to be reformatted."

A blue laser light the size of a golf ball emerged from his right hand.

"There she is Hank, his Crystal!" proclaimed Patrice.

"I see it!"

Jennifer appeared shock.

It moved.

First across his chest, around his torso, and then down his spine. It wrapped itself around his legs, feet, and arms, and then around his head.

Painting him with the blue light when all of a sudden, the light disappeared.

The man standing before them was no longer dressed in sneakers, torn jeans, nor a torn shirt, or jacket.

Daryl was now wearing black leather. Seam-lined with laser-blue light. Heavy black sneaker-soled biker boots. A black helmet, with an unreadable face.

On his chest glowed a blue 'L' with a subscript 'D' which also glowed blue.

Jennifer swallowed. "L-D?"

Henry whispered, broken, "Learning... disabled?"

The helmet tilted towards Henry.

"Incorrect dad," Daryl said.

And the light pulsed brighter.

Then the biker outfit faded away and Daryl stood there looking as if he had never been in a fight.

Daryl looked at his parents. "Why'd it take you so long to help me release Crystal?"

Patrice pointed at Henry,

"I told him we should have done it sooner!"

"You've got some 'splainin' to do," said Jennifer.

"The simplest answer," started Daryl, "is that I was born this way."

"No," Jennifer said as she shook her head, "your attacking me!"

"Yeah son," started Henry, "what was that about?"

"Well, I didn't know this until you woke Crystal and she updated my systems, but I was given two amputations I didn't need and when I got the prosthetics, the chip implanted into my brain which helped me to control the limbs was also used to control me."

"I'm sorry Jennifer, but if it weren't for you electrocuting me and shorting out that neural chip, they would've maintained control over me. Thank you!"

Jennifer nodded.

"And how were you able to electrocute him?" asked Patrice.

Jennifer smiled and put her hands close together, creating an electrical ark which buzzed and snapped.

"Now I done seen everything!" exclaimed Henry.

"My story is a bit complicated," started Jennifer, "but half the reason I am this way is because of that storm we were in and the other half is why we were struck by lightning in the first place."

"What?" asked Patrice

"None of that matters right now," started Daryl, "whether by accident or not, we've stumbled onto a major cover up in which people are getting mind controlled through the addition of prosthetic limbs, which they may or may not have needed. And I think maybe they intended to recruit you too."

"Why me?" asked Jennifer.

"We both survived the same lightning strike," started Daryl. "Someone figured out we were different, but at the same time, its probable that someone may have tried to keep you shielded."

"So what's the play?" asked Jennifer.

"We have to assume that they have soldiers, the thing is, we can't hurt them but we have to disable them."

"Destroying the chip will definitely stop them," started Jennifer, "but if that takes away their functional ability..."

"Many of them will feel as if they had their debilitating situation happen all over again," finished Daryl. "To some that would be worse than destroying them."

"So we take a different tact," said Jennifer.

"We already know that the orthopedic surgeons Park and Haines are involved."

"A neurosurgeon?"

"Doctor Nadia Feldman."

"Feldman?" asked Jennifer.

"You know her?" asked Daryl"

"Sort of, "started Jenifer, "she did my neuro exam prior to my discharge and when I thought I recognized her and asked her if we knew each other, she got all weird and said no. But when my dad reviewed my chart, he immediately recognized her name and said she used to come by our house when I was a child."

"Well weird or not, she was the one trying to keep you out of this, and she is the one who integrates the chip into the neuro system, so we need her."

"Now we just need a plan."

***

"The I.C.E. agents are at the location as ordered," started the technician. "The residence is empty."

Eleni nodded, unsurprised.

"Of course it is," she said.

She turned back to the frozen data on the screen.

"Dead," she repeated softly, amused.

"No..."

"No what?" asked Eleni.

"The woman is not there," started the technician and neither is Linard's body."

She picked up her tablet and walked toward the door.

"Could she have super strength and moved his body or is he somehow able to move despite damage to our chip?"

"He may be adapting," she said. "Bring me Feldman!"

"Of course," replied the technician.

TWELVE

JENNIFER AND DARYL opted not to enter the hospital through the front.

She parked two blocks away and approached on foot, keeping to the darker edges of the street, avoiding the main entrance where cameras watched everything.

He parked his motorcycle on the side of the hospital.

Jennifer's heart pounded as they connected. "What if she's already gone?"

Daryl glanced at her. "Then we keep looking for her until we find her and get her to help end this."

They slipped into the hospital through a side entrance near the loading dock. The hallway smelled like disinfectant and warm plastic.

Everything looked normal.

Which was the worst part.

They moved quickly, quietly, past a nurse's station, past an empty gurney, past a hallway where a television played softly in a waiting room.

Jennifer kept her hands in her jacket pockets.

Daryl noticed. "You okay?"

"I'm trying not to break anything," she murmured. Or create any unnecessary sparks. Oxygen and all."

Daryl almost smiled. "Good strategy."

They reached Neurology.

A receptionist sat behind a desk, half-asleep, eyes locked on whatever was on the computer.

Jennifer stepped forward. "Hi. We need to see Dr. Feldman."

The receptionist didn't look up. "She's gone for the night."

Daryl leaned in slightly. "I'm a patient of hers, are you certain I can't speak with her?"

The receptionist sighed and finally glanced up. "She signed out an hour ago."

Jennifer's stomach dropped.

Daryl's jaw tightened.

as she started to turn away, Jennifer caught something behind the receptionist's shoulder, a hallway light still on, deeper in the office wing. A door slightly ajar.

Jennifer forced a polite smile. "Okay. Thank you."

She turned away and whispered, "She's still here."

Daryl frowned. "How do you know?"

"The lights," Jennifer said. "Maybe she started to leave and came back, and Shannon here doesn't know."

Daryl didn't argue. He only followed.

They moved down the hallway toward the ajar door.

Jennifer knocked softly.

No answer.

She pushed the door open.

Dr. Feldman sat inside, coat off, sleeves rolled, staring at a computer screen as if she had been doing it for hours. She looked up, startled, then her face tightened.

"You," she said quietly.

Jennifer stepped in first. "Dr. Feldman."

Feldman's eyes flicked to Daryl.

Then to his limbs.

She didn't know if she was drunk or crazy but he looked as if he had his natural arm where his prosthetic should have been.

"What are you doing here?" Feldman asked.

Daryl shut the door behind them. "We need your help."

Feldman's expression hardened. "You need to leave."

Jennifer shook her head. "No. We need answers."

Feldman stood. "You don't understand what you're involved in."

Daryl took a step closer. "I understand enough to know you lied to me and many others. I also know there is good in you because you spared her," he said gesturing to Jennifer.

"We've never met before huh?" Jennifer smiled.

"Well, you were like five," suggested Feldman.

Feldman's jaw tightened as she looked at Daryl. "Look, I did what I had to do."

"You put something in my head," Daryl said. "And someone used it to make me attack her," another head point gesture towards Jennifer.

Feldman's eyes flashed.

For a moment, she said nothing. Then she exhaled slowly.

"You shouldn't have come here," she murmured.

Jennifer's heart raced. "Good people are being used as weapons of destruction, just because they wanted the ability to continue living a healthy, normal life."

Feldman looked away, like the ceiling had become suddenly interesting.

"Jennifer, your father is a good man," she said quietly. "That's why you're still walking."

Jennifer stared. "What's that supposed to mean?"

"It means I kept you out of it as long as I could," Feldman replied. "But you were struck in that storm. You survived. And now they know there is something special about you, just like him, and they want you."

"They?" Daryl asked. "Who are they?"

Feldman hesitated.

Then she looked at Daryl.

"The prosthetics weren't the real invention," she said. "The interface was. The ability to translate intention into movement... and movement into data."

Jennifer's hands clenched. "So they can track the users."

Feldman nodded. "Yes, but tracking is also a very small part of it. The prosthetics are bionic which augments the strength and speed of anyone who has them. The interface allows smooth use without lag or complications; the caveat is that the user can be controlled also."

Daryl's eyes narrowed as he took a breath. "I can't be tracked or controlled anymore."

Feldman blinked. "What?"

"My chip was damaged," Daryl said. "I'm off grid. However, when it was damaged, I felt like I was paralyzed again until I fixed myself."

Feldman stared at him like she didn't want to believe it.

Jennifer stepped closer. "The part of him fixing himself is a long story but the point is there are many others who cannot be helped in that way. Your interface is legendary and could truly help a lot of good people but right now that tech is in the wrong hands. Help us do the right thing," she said. "Not for us. For everyone who never needed those amputations."

Dr. Nadia Feldman's face tightened, caught between fear and conscience. "The cost of the prosthetics and the procedures is more than the cost the hospital or insurance companies can afford, so moving forward the program will have to be shut down."

"Damn," started Daryl.

"Even if I wanted to," she continued, "you don't understand what happens to people who betray Helix. They are far bigger than you know."

Jennifer's eyes hardened. "I don't care about Helix."

Daryl stepped back, voice calmer now. "Dr. Feldman... I'm not asking you to be brave forever. I'm asking you to be brave for the next twenty-four hours."

Feldman closed her eyes briefly. "No, you're asking me to be brave forever."

When she opened them, she looked exhausted.

"I signed out from work," she said quietly. "But I stayed because I couldn't sleep. Because I knew this day would come."

Jennifer swallowed. "Then come with us."

Feldman hesitated.

Then she nodded once.

"Alright," she said.

THIRTEEN

THEY DIDN'T MAKE it ten feet out of the office wing of the hospital before Jennifer felt it.

A shift in the air.

A faint electrical buzz, like static before a strike.

She stopped.

Daryl looked at her. "What?"

Jennifer's eyes widened. "They're here."

Before Daryl could respond, a voice echoed down the hallway, calm, mechanical.

"Dr. Dana Feldman."

Hearing her name froze her blood.

Two figures stepped into view at the far end of the corridor.

Matte-black uniforms. Face masks covering their faces from the nose down.

Feldman's breath hitched. "Oh no..."

Daryl's instincts flared. "Run."

Jennifer grabbed Feldman's wrist and pulled.

Daryl moved beside them, fast.

Behind them, the I.C.E. agents advanced with unhurried certainty.

Jennifer let go of Feldman as she felt panic try to rise, but something inside her pushed back harder.

The trio burst through a side stairwell.

Down two flights.

Out into the night.

Daryl's motorcycle waited where he left it, black and sleek, engine silent.

He looked at Jennifer. "You know where to meet us at!"

With that, Jennifer nodded, smiled, and took off into the sky as Feldman and other passers-by gasped in shock, watching her fly away.

Daryl's outfit phase shifted into the black biker uniform with the blue laser light trimming as his motorcycle also developed the blue laser light around the edges of the paneling and along the circumference of the rims.

His helmet, also with blue laser light starting at the chin and moving up and around where his ears would be and then zipping to the back, just appeared on his face as he hopped on the bike.

"Get on!" he shouted to Feldman.

Feldman hesitated only a second, then climbed behind him and held on as the bike roared to life.

As Jennifer flew, the air around her felt different now, thick, alive, like a current. This was her first time doing this outside of the confines of her home and she was loving it.

"Whoo yes!"

Jennifer's stomach dropped as she rose higher than she meant to. The wind slammed her hair back.

The hospital lights blurred far beneath her. Her heart thundered, but her body stayed up, suspended in invisible motion.

Ride the current.

She tilted slightly, and the air obeyed around her.

Below, Daryl was speeding on the motorcycle with Feldman clinging to him, tires yelling their song as they skimmed the road.

Jennifer shot forward above them, not flying like a bird but gliding like electricity itself, finding pathways in the wind, slipping into them, letting them carry her.

Then she saw the headlights.

One.

Two.

More.

Black vehicles emerging from side streets like they had been waiting.

***

Feldman looked over her shoulder and shouted something Daryl couldn't hear.

Assuming the worst, Daryl leaned forward, pushing the bike harder.

Two SUVS were coming up fast on Daryl and Feldman.

"I'M GONNA NEED YOU TO HOLD JUST A LITTLE BIT TIGHTER!"

Feldman complied.

Daryl popped a wheelie and when the front tire hit the ground the afterburners fired and the bike sped up, bobbing and weaving through the traffic as car horns blared and as two of the SUVs maintained pursuit.

One of the SUVs was leading and the passenger climbed halfway out the window and started firing a semi-automatic weapon in the direction of Daryl and Feldman.

"SHIELD'S UP!" yelled Daryl as a translucent blue light immediately circled the motorcycle, causing bullets to bounce off of them as Feldman screamed.

From high above, Jenifer shot an electric beam around the second SUV, causing it to be picked up and thrown to the side and onto its side.

Jennifer laughed as she looked at her hand.

"Electromagnetism? New power unlocked!"

She flew forward

Down on the road, the I.C.E. agent passed his gun into the car window and climbed all the way out the window and slammed his titanium hand into the roof of the car, securing his grip and he then pulled himself onto the roof of the speeding SUV.

He then stood up.

The agent jumped up and forward from off the SUV with the intent to come down onto the motorcycle, but he was ambushed by Jennifer who grabbed him and flew him off course.

The agent started reaching behind and swatting her with his metal arm to ty to get her to let go.

"I promise Daryl," she started to herself as she swayed left and right while carrying him, "I'll just give him one little shock!"

She jolted the agent with electricity and then quickly lowered him to the ground.

The agent's eyes closed.

"That was way less juice than I used on Daryl," she shook her head in the affirmative. "He'll be okay!"

She then took to the sky again.

Daryl and Feldman were making ground with the shield still around them and losing the one SUV with the other still following them.

All of a sudden, Daryl reached behind to Feldman with his right hand and tossed her straight up into the air.

She screamed as she flew upward and watched below in horror as Daryl was Broadsided by a third SUV.

Daryl flew hard off the bike due to the impact and was thrown twenty yards as the motorcycle was totaled, smashed into a multitude of fragments.

As gravity started to reclaim Feldman, Jennifer grabbed her and then flew off in a northern direction. *Stick to the plan*, she thought.

Jennifer's eyes narrowed as she looked back at Daryl.

More I.C.E. agents were joining the scene.

Stick to the plan, she again thought to herself as Feldman stopped screaming and started crying.

And for the first time, Jennifer understood something clearly:

Whatever Helix was, it was bigger than she realized.

And they had just pushed their buttons.

***

As they pulled up, the I.C.E. agents all emptied out of their SUVs and started to circle Daryl as he picked himself up off the ground.

There were a lot of them. Men, women, black, white, Asian, all of them wearing the same thing, all black from shoulder to toe and a silver face mask which came down from their nose over their chin and neck.

Daryl looked at his damaged motorcycle and then looked around at the small number of I.C.E. agents he was about to engage into combat with.

"Eighteen?" he asked disappointedly as he cracked his neck, "maybe I should've asked Jen to wait for me after all! Crystal!"

The golf-sized glowing ball emerged from his chest as the agents started to move in on him.

"Can you fix my bike while I take care of these guys?"

Right away! Crystal immediately went on to fix the bike.

"Try to win the fight without damaging their neural chips. There's a ninety seven percent probability that I can take them all down!" Daryl said out loud and to himself.

The first agent lunged.

Daryl stepped *into* the attack.

A gloved fist came at his face; he slipped it by inches and drove his forearm into the agent's sternum, not hard enough to crush, just hard enough to knock the breath out of him. The agent folded, stunned but alive.

Two more rushed him from opposite sides.

Daryl jumped.

Not high, *fast*.

He twisted midair, kicking one agent in the chest while hammering the other with an elbow to the shoulder joint.

Simultaneously, the blue light grabbed pieces of the motorcycle and started pulling them closer to each other in proximity.

The impact sent the second agent skidding across the pavement, armor scraping, with sparks flickering from underneath, but intact.

"Four down," Daryl muttered.

The circle tightened.

Simultaneously, the motorcycle started looking like a motorcycle as the blue light continued restoring parts.

The remaining agents adapted immediately.

Three agents withdrew compact batons from behind which hummed to life, red electricity rippling along their length.

Another agent raised a wrist-mounted launcher.

Daryl dove just as a net of electrified filament snapped shut where he had been standing. It crackled angrily against the asphalt.

"Nice trick," he said, rolling to his feet.

In his background, the glowing rimmed tires of the motorcycle moved into place."

Daryl sprinted straight towards the launcher agent.

The agent fired again.

Daryl slid under it, came up inside the agent's reach, and ripped the launcher clean off the man's arm. He crushed it in his hand and tossed it aside.

A baton struck his back.

Hard.

The impact rang through his spine, sending a cascade of warning signals through his limbs. Daryl grunted but stayed upright.

"Okay," he growled. "That one counts."

He turned and grabbed the baton mid-swing, wrenching it from the agent's grip. With a precise twist, he jabbed the butt end into the agent's neck, *not* the spine, just the pressure point.

The agent collapsed instantly.

Six down.

The rest didn't rush anymore.

They moved like a unit now, calculating angles, spacing, overlapping fields of attack.

Daryl looked from left to right.

"Crystal," he said under his breath. "Analysis."

Opponents exhibit synchronized combat algorithms. Recommend disruption.

"Yeah," Daryl said. "I had the same conclusion."

He slammed his right foot into the ground.

The pavement *cracked*.

A shockwave rippled outward, throwing two agents off their feet and staggering three more. Daryl charged through the opening, weaving, striking, disabling wrists, knees, shoulders, always precise, always controlled.

An agent vaulted onto his back.

Daryl reached over his shoulder, grabbed the agent's arm, and flipped him clean over his head. The agent hit the ground hard and didn't move.

Ten.

Another agent came in low with a sweep.

Daryl jumped again, but this time an agent clipped his leg midair.

He hit the ground rolling.

Before he could rise, two agents pinned him, one on each arm, while a third raised a baton for a finishing strike.

"No," Daryl snapped.

The blue light on his outfit flared.

Not outward.

Inward.

His limbs surged with controlled power. He pushed up from the ground, lifting *all three* agents with him. He slammed them down in opposite directions, the baton skittering across the asphalt.

He stood.

Breathing hard now.

Four agents left.

They hesitated.

That was their mistake.

Daryl moved like lightning, faster than thought, faster than fear. He disarmed one, dropped another with a shoulder strike, then caught the last two mid-charge.

He smacked their heads together.

They went limp instantly.

Silence fell.

Daryl stood alone in the wreckage, breathing hard, leather slightly shredded but immediately repaired with blue light

He looked around.

Eighteen agents.

All down.

All alive.

Crystal finished repairing the motorcycle behind him, panels sliding back into place with a soft mechanical hum as the bike started.

"Thanks," Daryl said, walking towards the bike.

As he swung a leg over the bike, he paused and glanced back at the unconscious agents.

"You all deserve better than this," he said quietly.

The engine roared to life.

Blue light traced the edges of the bike as Daryl accelerated into the night, leaving behind broken asphalt, unanswered questions...

...and a war which had just begun.

FOURTEEN

THE ROOM WAS lit only by the glow of screens.

Dozens of them.

Chest cams. Wrist-mounted telemetry feeds. Each window showed a fragment of the same night; chaos fractured into angles and data points.

The Helix Systems technician scrubbed backward through the footage.

"Playback synced," he said quietly.

Eleni Kallistratos stood behind him, arms folded, posture relaxed. She looked less like a general overseeing a battlefield and more like someone reviewing a quarterly report.

On-screen, an I.C.E. agent rounded a corner at a dead run.

Then the camera jolted violently upward.

"Pause," Eleni said.

The image froze.

Jennifer Harding hovered in the air.

Her body was angled slightly forward, hair whipping around her face, electricity crawling over her arms in visible arcs. She didn't fly like something with wings, she rode the air as if it belonged to her, as if she had discovered a rule everyone else had missed.

The technician swallowed. "That's... her."

"Yes," Eleni replied calmly. "Enhance."

The image sharpened.

Another feed popped up beside it, this one from a different agent.

A mysterious figure stood in the middle of the roadway.

Not injured. Not panicked.

Waiting.

He wore black leather lined with laser-blue seams that pulsed faintly with movement. His helmet reflected a multitude of headlights and gunfire alike, unreadable. His limbs moved with precision which bordered on contempt.

His motorcycle totaled.

The technician shook his head. "That suit isn't in our database."

"No," Eleni said. "It wouldn't be."

They watched as the figure engaged.

He didn't rush.

They observed a strange blue light and the mysterious self-repair of the totaled motorcycle.

The figure stepped inside attacks. Redirected strikes. Disarmed agents with movements so efficient they looked rehearsed. He slammed one operative into the pavement and rolled seamlessly into the next without breaking stride.

Another previous occurrence feed flared.

Dr. Nadia Feldman clung to Daryl's back as the motorcycle tore down the street, shield flaring blue as bullets sparked harmlessly away.

Then—

Daryl reached back.

The technician leaned forward. "What is he..."

On-screen, Daryl *threw* Feldman upward.

The footage jumped as the agent wearing the cam staggered in surprise.

Jennifer streaked down from above, caught Feldman mid-fall, and carried her skyward in a controlled arc that looked almost graceful.

The technician exhaled sharply. "Jesus..."

The feeds continued.

SUVs overturned. Agents incapacitated, cleanly. Deliberately. No excessive force. No crushed skulls. No torn hardware.

The motorcycle was now fully repaired.

Finally, the last helmet cam went dark.

Silence filled the room.

The technician stared at the summary panel as it populated.

"Twenty-two agents were actually deployed for this debacle," he said. "Eighteen incapacitated by Linard. Four by Harding."

He paused. "None of the neural chips were damaged. Not one. Prosthetics are intact across the board."

Eleni's lips curved, not into a smile, exactly, but something close.

"Efficiency," she said. "Restraint. Control."

The technician glanced back at her. "That shouldn't be possible."

"And yet," Eleni replied, "it is. If that truly is Linard, there's no way he should be walking around let alone fighting that well with a damaged chip in his head." She nodded.

"He is something else, they are both something else as I thought," she agreed with herself. "Something about that storm may have changed them both, but why so drastically? Maybe I've got it all wrong, but they are exactly what I need flying my flag."

She stepped closer to the screen showing Jennifer suspended in the air, lightning coiling around her like a living thing.

"She's definitely more than what I've projected," Eleni murmured. "Much more."

"And Linard?" the technician asked.

Eleni's gaze shifted to the frozen image of the dark figure standing alone in the street, surrounded by fallen I.C.E. agents.

"He's no longer ours," she said. "But he's still useful. If we can obtain him, I am certain we can regain control. I would still like to know how he is able to use our prosthetics without us being able to detect them."

She straightened.

"Where did they go?"

The technician pulled up another screen. "Traffic cameras lost them near the river."

"They have Feldman," she started, "Let Rourke and the others know that Feldman's been compromised and there will be no more surgeries at Heritage until we find her and take care of those two nuisances. Order the retrieval of our fallen agents back to Helix for patch up and reintegration until they are needed further."

He tapped a few keys on the keyboard.

"DAMN!" she snapped as she slammed a fist on the table in front of her.

***

The Monongahela Crest Hotel sat along a winding stretch of highway, overlooking a forested valley. The building was older but well-kept, with stone accents and warm interior lighting that contrasted with the isolation of its surroundings.

As Daryl drove down the darkened highway, and as he made sure, he wasn't being followed, his outfit shifted from his costume back to his street clothes and the blue lights on his motorcycle faded.

He then pulled into the parking lot of the hotel, developing a sigh of relief seeing his parents' car there as well.

Daryl then parked the motorcycle, hopped off the bike and made his way to the hotel room.

Inside of the hotel, it felt quietly forgotten, comfortable, but unremarkable.

A place travelers stayed without drawing attention.

The lobby smelled faintly of coffee and wood polish. The rooms were clean, simple, and insulated from outside noise.

It was the kind of place people chose when they didn't want to be found.

Room one twelve, he thought as he made his way around the hotel until he found it. He then knocked on the door once.

He paused.

He knocked once again.

Again, a pause.

He then knocked twice.

This time the door opened, and Daryl walked in and immediately noticed that Feldman was laying on the couch holding a damp towel over her midsection.

"What happened?"

"I accidently burned her while carrying her, " started Jennifer.

"You didn't have the suit on under your clothes?"

"Yes I had the suit," she snapped, "you don't think I would wear the suit? I knew contact burns was a possibility."

Daryl walked over to Dr. Feldman. "Let me take a look."

Feldman winced. "It's only a small burn."

Daryl pulled back the damp towel and saw the damaged skin. "These are second degree burns!"

"I know," she exclaimed "I don't think the suit I had on under my clothes was good enough."

Daryl held out his palm and again produced the blue golf ball sized spere of light and passed it over Feldman's abdomen. "Crystal, restructure her abdominal wound to original status.

These are second degree burns, shouldn't be a problem!

After several passes over the abdomen, the wound was gone.

Feldman looked up at Daryl amazed.

"It may take a few minutes for your body to register before the pain subsides," said Daryl.

"You can heal people?" asked Jennifer.

"I can heal people?" asked Daryl. "No, no, it's not exactly like that...hand me your suit."

"You sort of looked like you healed her," started Jennifer as she passed him the suit.

"I look and am feeling much better," agreed Feldman.

Daryl took the suit and looked at it closely. Your suit has dielectric insulation."

"Yes, I know," started Jennifer, "I crafted it myself! Even under my regular clothing, it should've worked."

"You need a mid-layer Faraday mesh," started Daryl, "it'll prevent you from accidentally shocking or burning people when you touch them."

"A mid-layer Faraday mesh?" asked Jennifer.

Daryl nodded yes.

"Why didn't I think of that?"

Feldman looked up at Daryl curiously. "You could barely do serial seven when I did your neuro exam, how do you know about Faraday?"

"Long story," they both answered simultaneously.

"You should also do better at concealing your identity if you're going to make it a habit of flying around the city."

Jennifer sucked her teeth, "I'm not gonna make flying a habit!"

"Crystal,"

The glowing sphere reappeared.

"Take this suit, upgrade to advanced dielectric insulation and add a mid-layer Faraday mesh,"

Let her know I will need to take measurements also.

"She will need to take your measurements also," added Daryl. He then smiled. "Give her a Lazer Droid upgrade!"

Your wish is my command dot com!

Daryl laughed.

The spherical light circled Jennifer multiple times and then passed through the front of her forehead and exited the back of her head.

The sphere then danced around the body suit Daryl was holding, transforming it structurally and aesthetically.

76

The suit then vanished.

"Hey, where'd my body suit go?"

"She linked it to your powers and your mind; all you have to do now is will it to be on you."

Jennifer closed her eyes.

Electricity crackled all over her body and her street clothes changed into something else.

When her metamorphosis was complete, Jennifer stood with a commanding, grounded posture, feet planted shoulder-width apart, as if she was bracing herself against a powerful force, or daring it to strike.

Her physique was athletic and sculpted, conveying strength without bulk, agility without fragility. Every line of her stance suggested control, confidence, and readiness.

She wore a full-body, form-fitting suit constructed from a sleek, high-tech material which appeared both flexible and armored. The base color was a deep, matte black, absorbing light rather than reflecting it, giving her a shadowed, almost predatory silhouette. Threaded throughout the suit were glowing electric-blue conduits which traced the contours of her body, along her arms, legs, torso, and spine, like living circuits or veins of energy.

The illuminated lines pulsed subtly, implying the suit was not merely decorative but actively channeling her power.

At the center of her chest, the glow intensified into a concentrated emblem-like convergence, which was shaped organically rather than symbolically, as if the energy originated from within her rather than being imposed upon her.

The focal point radiated outward in branching lines, reinforcing the impression she was both the source and the conduit of the electricity surrounding her.

Her hands were clenched loosely at her sides, fingers slightly curled, crackling arcs of blue-white electricity leaping between her knuckles and palms.

She wore a sleek, angular visor which covered her eyes, glowing faintly with the same electric-blue hue as the energy in her suit. The mask obscured her gaze while amplifying her mystique, giving her an unreadable, intimidating presence.

Her blond hair flowed freely around her shoulders, caught in an unseen current. Strands lifted and rippled as if stirred by static electricity or a charged atmosphere.

"Whoa," said Jennifer.

"Wow," agreed Feldman.

"I think your name should be Kalelectra," started Daryl.

"Kalelectra?" asked Jennifer.

"Kalos from the Greek word meaning beauty," started Daryl "And electra obviously because of your abilities."

Jennifer smiled. "I like that...Kalelectra!"

"So you can make things and heal people?" asked Feldman.

Jennifer changed back into her alter ego. "He healed himself when his chip was damaged and he could no longer use the leg or arm you gave him."

"How did you get the leg and arm to work if the chip was damaged?" asked Feldman. "And why do they now have synthetic skin over them?"

Daryl sat down on the sofa. "I can't make things, I can only alter what's already there. Like my bike, I didn't make it, I only altered it. Your suit Jennifer...altered."

"What about your leg and arm, they look like you grew them back?"

"Altered," started Daryl, "Crystal helped me reformat my body so that the myelion neurotitanium has been infused into my DNA and blended with my whole body."

"So are you a man or a robot?" asked Jenifer.

"He's an android," said Feldman.

Daryl nodded, I am like an android, hence the name..."

"Lazer Droid," interjected Jennifer smilingly. "I heard you say it a little while ago."

"No wonder you were able to integrate into our systems so well," started Feldman. "You were like a biological robot."

"What is Crystal?" asked Jennifer. "And why can't we hear her?"

"Crystal is like my, how do you say it here? My soulmate. I reincarnated on earth by accident and she became what you would call an angel. The blue light you see with me now is a part of her soul watching over me."

The two women appeared stunned.

"When I was born, somehow, what I was before carried over to my new life...I suspect it was Crystal's doing...my ability to process and interpret information scared my parents and they didn't know how to deal with me. They loved me, but they feared what would happen to me if anyone ever found out what I was able to do so I locked away my memories and gave them a key to unlock me as an adult and I suppressed my memories with Crystal being my key."

"Them holding you back caused you to be..."

"No," interrupted Daryl, "Everything happens for a reason, and I believe we were truly put on this path to come to this moment!"

They both looked at Dr. Feldman.

"What?" she asked.

FIFTEEN

THE ROOM WAS quiet again.

Not the brittle silence of fear, but the heavier kind, the kind which came after decisions had already been made.

Dr. Nadia Feldman sat on the edge of the hotel couch, shoulders slumped, hands wrapped around a cooling mug of coffee she half consumed.

Her eyes were fixed on the carpet as though it might give her permission to speak.

Daryl leaned against the far wall, arms crossed, his reflection faint in the darkened window.

Jennifer stood near the door, restless, electricity humming just beneath her skin like a held breath.

"They won't stop," Feldman said finally.

No one answered her at first.

"They'll pause," she continued. "They'll change coding language. Change funding routes. But Helix doesn't shut down, it migrates." She looked up at Daryl then. "Eleni designed it that way."

Daryl nodded slowly. "So we don't burn it down."

"Then we take out Eleni," suggested Jennifer.

"There will just be another Eleni waiting in line," Daryl replied as Feldman nodded in agreement.

"No," Feldman said. "You can't just...take her out."

Jennifer folded her arms. "Then what *can* we do?"

Feldman exhaled. "We cut the leash."

She reached into her bag and pulled out a small data drive, setting it carefully on the table between them.

"There's a synchronization window," she said. "Short. Dangerous. But real. During it, the I.C.E. neural chips receive subconscious command updates. These updates help keep them in line and compliant." She looked at Daryl. "That's also when control is strongest."

"Or weakest," he said.

"Yes," she admitted. "If someone permanently interrupts the signal, someone Helix can't possibly gain control of if caught, they could sever the command layer without destroying the hardware in the candidates."

Jennifer frowned. "You're talking about freeing them. No more I.C.E. agents?"

"I'm talking about giving them a choice," Feldman corrected. "Some won't take it."

Daryl closed his eyes briefly, then nodded once. "That's still better than slavery."

Feldman swallowed. "If we do this, there's no going back for me."

Jennifer met her gaze. "There wasn't anyway."

A faint, sad smile touched Feldman's lips. "I stayed because I hoped someone like you would come."

She stood.

"I can get you in," she said. "Once."

Daryl pushed off the wall. "Then that's enough. Ready Kalelectra?"

Jennifer smiled. "Hell yeah!"

***

Helix Systems did not look like a place meant to be invaded.

The compound rose from the industrial outskirts like a cathedral of glass and steel, clean lines, soft lighting, landscaped barriers meant to signal *order*, not secrecy. A tall fence around the perimeter, but no razor wire. No guard towers. Just confidence.

As they walked along the dark trail, wearing basic black purchased with cash earlier at a local Walmart, Daryl couldn't help to be in awe of the sight they were taking in. "Whoa," he said modestly."

"That's how you know it's dangerous," Jennifer murmured.

Daryl didn't answer. His eyes were fixed on the building's upper levels, where the synchronization core lived, where time itself was sliced into windows and exploited.

As they walked along the fence, Feldman spotted a door. "There it is!" she exclaimed.

Daryl picked up Feldman as if he were about to carry her over a threshold and nodded at Jennifer.

He then leapt effortlessly over the fence as she floated upward and over it.

She then landed as Daryl lowered Feldman to the ground and they headed over to a obscure metal door.

They entered through the service access door which Feldman recognized, having reviewed schematics in the past and making sure she knew every nook and cranny in case she ever had to make an escape.

The first guard barely had time to register surprise before Daryl disarmed him, twisted, and pinned him to the wall. Jennifer dropped the second with a pulse of electricity precise enough to overload the suit but leave his body and chip intact.

They moved fast.

Almost too fast.

Helix's interior was colder than the night outside, white corridors, soft hums, the sound of machines breathing.

Every step taken with deliberation and moving them closer to the core.

The anxiety felt like pressure building within Jennifer's skull, *I wish I could just fry them all and be done with it*, she thought to herself.

"They're cycling early," Feldman said, glancing at her watch. "The window's opening."

That's when the alarm *didn't* sound.

Instead, a single guard, wounded but conscious, reached up and pressed two fingers to the upper right side of his face mask.

A signal went out.

***

Eleni Kallistratos' condo overlooked the city from a height which made everything below feel abstract.

At night, the glass walls turned the skyline into a living mosaic, streams of headlights threading through streets like veins of light, windows flickering on and off in distant buildings, the river reflecting it all in broken silver lines. From up here, people looked small. Predictable. Manageable.

The interior of the condo was dim by design.

No overhead lights. Only carefully placed illumination, low amber strips along the floor, recessed lighting behind shelves, the soft glow of screens embedded seamlessly into walls and furniture. The effect was intentional: nothing harsh, nothing accidental. Shadows existed only where she allowed them.

The space itself was immaculate but not sterile. Modern lines, polished stone floors, dark wood accents. Furniture arranged with precision rather than comfort, chairs meant to be sat in briefly, not lounged upon.

There were no personal photographs, no sentimental clutter. The few decorative objects present were abstract sculptures and framed technical schematics rendered as art.

A place designed to impress no one.

At one end of the condo, a wide console faced the windows, its surface alive with quiet data streams, security feeds, system diagnostics, regional reports scrolling in disciplined columns.

A half-empty glass of red wine sat untouched nearby.

The city thundered faintly below, sirens, distant traffic, the restless noise of millions of lives colliding, but none of it reached her. The soundproofing was flawless.

Eleni preferred it that way.

From this height, she didn't need to hear the city to understand it. She watched patterns, not people. Systems, not souls.

When her phone finally vibrated on the console, the sound felt sharp in the quiet space.

She woke before the phone finished vibrating.

Eleni got up and stood there barefoot, dressed in black silk which caught the low light like liquid shadow, one hand resting lightly on the edge of nightstand as she reviewed the information coming through on her pager without urgency.

She didn't look confused. She didn't ask questions.

She was already sitting up, already reaching for the tablet on her nightstand on the other side of the telephone.

Her lover tonight, naked, silent, eyes unfocused, laid calmy in bed, waiting until the moment she touched his chip interface.

"Dress," she said.

He moved.

"They're inside," she continued calmly, already getting dressed as he did the same. "We need to secure all three, Harding and Linard alive, I don't care what happens to Feldman, on second thought, we can still use that big brain of hers, we will integrate her in some way."

She smiled faintly as she placed a watch looking device on her wrist and pressed a small button on the side.

"Yes maam?" asked the Technician.

"I need a mass closest to proximity mobilized to Helix...NOW! she ordered.

"Directly!" replied the technician.

***

The door to the core chamber weighed half a ton but opened silently after Daryl pushed it open.

Inside, the room curved like an amphitheater. Servers pulsed with blue-white light, cables ran like veins into the floor, and at the center stood the synchronization pillar, alive with data, timing, control.

Feldman ran for it.

Her hands shook as she slammed the USB drive into the port and an automatic keyboard slid outward.

Feldman immediately started typing.

"Once this starts," she said, breathless, "there's no stopping it."

"Do it," Jennifer said.

The upload began and simultaneously, a download started onto the drive, updating information Feldman didn't yet know about.

All across Pennsylvania, and beyond, something broke.

Prosthetic recipients, previous Helix Systems candidates, awoke suddenly from their sleep if they were asleep, becoming aware of all the information once hidden from them.

Out on the town being social and becoming aware.

Sitting in their apartment all alone, becoming aware.

Checking in on their sleeping children and becoming aware.

Some discovering suitcases containing an outfit under their beds collapsing and sobbing.

Some enraged, smashing walls, punching concrete, memories slamming through of all of their subconscious activities, everything coming back all at once. Others. Trained, hardened, suddenly felt clarity return and understood immediately *who* had done this.

And where it occurred.

Some, who felt grateful and willing to follow the next command. *Go to Helix and capture Harding, Feldman, and Linard, at any cost!*

Those appreciative recipients garbed up and took his/her own personal oath to defend Helix Systems.

And of those participants, those even closest to Helix prepared to run towards it.

SIXTEEN

BY THE TIME Daryl yanked Feldman away from the terminal, the halls were no longer empty.

They poured in.

I.C.E. agents, dozens of them, then more, no longer synchronized, no longer restrained. Some fought wildly. Others moved with lethal precision born of *choice*, not command.

"This wasn't supposed to happen," Feldman whispered.

"Uh...," Daryl grunted. "This was always the risk."

They burst into the halls and stopped.

An army waited.

Not marching. Not uniform.

Individuals.

People who had *chosen* Helix.

Jennifer felt it immediately, the difference. No static hesitation. No hesitation at all.

a bullet moved quickly towards Daryl as the blue sphere exited his chest, and quickly formed a blue translucent shield, stopping the bullet's path.

Daryl turned to Feldman. "Stay down!"

"What?" she asked.

He phased his costume into place, black leather replacing his gear from toe to neck, helmet appearing as well The blue lasers lit up directly. "So much for stealth!"

Lightening flashed in the hall as Jennifer started elevating upward, changing her gear into her costume, changing into Kalelectra!

Kalelectra descended beside him, electricity rolling over her like a living storm.

They didn't exchange words.

They didn't need to.

The agents came in waves.

This time, there was no time for restraint.

Kalelectra took a blade across the ribs and screamed but stayed aloft as she jolted the offending I.C.E. agent, rendering him unconscious.

Daryl caught a baton to the shoulder and then to his face causing a large open crack to the mask.

Blood from Kalelectra hit the floor as the cut to her abdomen healed and the costume sealed up.

Blue light dimmed around Lazer Droid's helmet and the crack to the mask sealed shut, then the lights flared again.

Lazer Droid and Kalelectra fought like they knew the stakes, and they did.

Kalelectra knew the soft spots and when the angry I.C.E. agents came at them with extreme prejudice, she jolted their chips, enough to subdue, but not enough to damage, her control of her abilities, increasing.

Her measures necessary at this point.

Lazer Droid couldn't help himself, he had a moral code which was engrained in him, *take down, no loss of life!*

His own potential Achilles' Heel.

By the time the battle ended, bodies lay everywhere, some unconscious, but everyone breathing.

The price of freedom was written in silence and smoke.

"Dr. Feldman!" called Lazer Droid as he extended his hand back towards her.

Feldman emerged from a hallway and ran over to the pair as they proceeded to exit the building.

Thirty seconds after they stepped out of the side entrance, flood lights flashed over them, and they could see what looked to be an army standing before them.

Lazer Droid whistled sharply.

The laser light embedded Kawasaki Ninja came flying over the fence well over the heads of the multitude of I.C.E. agents.

The bike then landed and turned around one hundred and eighty degrees upon reaching the trio.

"Get on the bike!" Lazer Droid barked at Feldman.

"What?!"she asked nervously and then quickly complied.

"How'd you whistle through the helmet?" asked Kalelectra.

Daryl just looked at her as she shrugged. "Crystal!"

The blue laser lit orb emerged from his chest.

"Convert the bike to flight mode with forcefield and get Dr. Feldman out of here!"

The blue orb immediately complied and started transforming the motorcycle into a flight vehicle and as the first bullets approached her, the shields went up around Feldman, deflecting them.

The bike with Feldman on it, then took off!

Two I.C.E. agents with jetpacks immediately took off after them as Lazer Droid and Kalelectra looked up.

"They've really got resources," spouted Kalelectra as electricity crackled around her hands and as she elevated. "Oh no you don't!" She then took off after them.

Lazer Droid looked down and ahead of him as he heard an I.C.E. agent speak for the first time, no longer subdued by mind control an inevitable wild card amongst a bunch of them.

"And then there was one," said the agent.

Lazer Droid laughed. "Trust me, I'm enough!"

The agents all charged him as he ran and jumped up and into the crowd.

***

The two agents flew fast after the bike as Kalelectra caught up to one of them and put her hands on his jet pack.

The agent looked at her as he kept flying. "Hey cutie, mind if I see how this works?"

She then jolted it with electricity as the straps caught fire and the engine burned out. the straps then broke and the agent fell screaming to the ground.

"Awe, this doesn't work!" she said as she dropped it and went after the other agent.

The other agent, oblivious to what happened to his partner continued to shoot at Feldman as Kalelectra gained on him. "We can't have you learning where we're hiding," she said out loud and to herself."

She then threw an electromagnetic rope around the agent catching him by surprise and causing him to drop his gun, as she made him turn to face her.

The electricity shorted out the jet pack and black smoke soon came from its seems.

Her facial expression turned into one of anger. "You're choosing to do this!"

The agent swung his metal fist towards her.

She let go of him and shot him with a large beam of electricity as he fell to the ground.

His body shook violently after hitting the asphalt.

She looked down at him satisfied. "We liberated you, you ungrateful bitch!"

She then took off back to Lazer Droid.

***

Lazer Droid took a baton to the back of the head and started to fall forward but then a punch to the face sent him flying back and as he flew, his hands touched the ground, and he spring boarded up into a fighting stance.

Bullets bombarded him but bounced off as a large jolt of electricity barreled down on his assailant.

Kalelectra descended facing him.

"You still wanna spare lives?" she asked.

"I most certainly do," he said.

"That guy was about to kill you!"

"I'm bullet proof," he started. "You know, for a doctor, you've really got some anger management issues!"

They both went in to take care of the remaining attackers.

They moved together.

Not side by side, *interlaced*.

The next wave of I.C.E. agents came fast, no hesitation now, no formation. These weren't drones anymore. These were people who made decisions.

Two charged Lazer Droid head-on, batons humming with red electricity, while three more broke wide, angling for Kalelectra.

Lazer Droid met the first with a shoulder which cracked armor and sent the agent spinning into the concrete wall hard enough to leave a spiderweb fracture behind him upon impact. He caught the second mid-swing, twisted the baton free, and snapped it across his knee like kindling.

Kalelectra didn't wait.

She darted upward and then suddenly dropped from above like a lightning strike, landing between three agents with a concussive electromagnetic pulse which blew them backward in a ring of shattered asphalt and scattered sparks.

One agent slammed back into a support column and didn't get back up.

Another agent rose back up, screaming, and charging blindly.

Kalelectra caught him by the vest and hurled him with an electric shove up and over the fence with strength she didn't know she had, into the barren roadway.

"Not to shabby," she said as she admired her arms.

An agent behind her fired.

Lazer Droid moved without thinking.

He crossed the distance in a blur, caught the projectile mid-air, and crushed it in his palm before it detonated. The recoil shuddered through his arm, blue light flaring as microfractures sealed instantly.

"Kalelectra!" he barked.

She turned just in time to see an agent vault over a railing above her, coming down with both feet aimed at her spine.

Lazer Droid jumped.

He hit the agent mid-descent, carried the momentum through the fall, and slammed him into the asphalt hard enough to knock the air out of both of them.

The agent tried to rise.

Lazer Droid pinned him with one hand.

"Stop!" Lazer Droid said, not pleading. Commanding.

The agent tried resisting.

Lazer Droid punched him in the face, rendering him unconscious.

Twenty feet away, Kalelectra wasn't so restrained.

A female agent caught her face by surprise, and clipped her, sending her skidding and screaming across the asphalt in a spray of sparks and blood.

She rolled, came up on one knee, breath ragged, visor flashing white at the edges.

That did it.

She screamed, not in fear, but rage, and the lights above them shattered as electricity surged outward in jagged arcs. Two agents were lifted clean off their feet, elevated two hundred feet up, and dropped unconscious into smoking heaps.

Lazer Droid felt the surge ripple through his systems.

"KALELECTRA!"

"I KNOW!" she shouted back. "NO KILLING. I know!"

The last three attackers regrouped, wounded but determined.

They rushed together.

Lazer Droid met them head-on.

Kalelectra flanked.

No flourish. No hesitation.

Lazer Droid disarmed one, as his optics identified the real knee of another and shattered it with a precise kick, and drove the third into the wall of a building with a blow which stopped just short of lethal force.

Kalelectra finished it, one sharp, controlled discharge that dropped all three where they stood.

Silence followed.

Not sudden.

Earned.

Smoke curled upward.

Broken limbs whirled softly as bionics of the fallen had powered down.

The courtyard and parking lot combined looked like it had been chewed apart by something angry and deliberate.

Kalelectra stood there, chest heaving, blood streaked across her side, electricity still crawling over her visible skin in restless veins.

Lazer Droid straightened slowly, adrenaline boost finally quieting.

"Crystal, my overall systems integrity?"

You have only been compromised by eleven percent.

"Why does it feel like so much more?"

"What did she say?" asked Kalelectra.

"That I am forty-three percent damaged," Lazer Droid lied.

That is not what I said!

They looked at each other.

No smiles.

Both with questions.

Kalelectra wiped blood from her mouth with the back of her hand and let out a breath she hadn't realized she was holding.

"We're done," she said.

Lazer Droid nodded.

"Can I get a lift?" he asked.

She stood close behind him and grabbed him from under the arms, and they flew up and into the night, looking like a bright star.

Behind them, Helix Systems began to fracture, not explode, not collapse, but crack.

At the moment, cracks were enough.

SEVENTEEN

THE HOTEL ROOM was quiet in the way only exhaustion could create.

Jennifer sat cross-legged on the edge of the bed, her suit phased down to civilian clothes, sleeves rolled up, faint scratch marks still visible along her forearm.

Daryl stood near the window, arms folded, staring out at the parking lot below as if keeping watch over a world that didn't know how close it had come to tearing itself apart.

Dr. Feldman hadn't stopped working.

She sat at the small desk by the window, laptop open, the glow of the screen painting sharp lines across her face.

The USB drive lay beside the keyboard, unscathed, still warm from the transfer.

"I don't get it," started Daryl, "We know she's building an army; we know how she's building the army, but we don't know the why. What's her endgame?"

"Yeah," agreed Jennifer. "Why even build an army."

"I don't like this," Feldman muttered.

Daryl turned to her. "What?"

She didn't look up. Her fingers moved faster now, pulling up layered directories, code within code, buried protocols which hadn't appeared in the primary Helix architecture.

"They segmented the system," she said. "Not just redundancies. Compartmentalization."

Jennifer frowned. "Meaning?"

"Meaning we saw what they *wanted* us to see." Feldman's heart sunk. "They didn't think the chip core could ever be breeched, so it wasn't hidden. But we left something important untouched."

Daryl stepped closer. The air around him felt different, subtle, charged, the way it always did when Crystal was paying attention from within.

Feldman stopped typing.

For a long moment, she simply stared at the screen.

"No," she whispered.

Jennifer rose to her feet. "What'd you find?"

Feldman turned the laptop toward them.

A schematic filled the display, an underground wing branching off Helix's main complex.

No public access points.

No logged personnel movement.

Shielded power grid.

And one active life-support signature.

"A holding ward," Feldman said quietly. "Medical, but not surgical. No ortho prep. No integration protocols."

Daryl's eyes narrowed. "Then why keep her sedated?"

Feldman zoomed in on the patient file.

CERHESS, SORRIE — Age 29
Status: Stable. Induced coma.
**Evaluation Notes: *Deferred. Observation only.* **

Jennifer's breath caught.

"Sorrie Cerhess," she said softly.

Daryl turned sharply. "You know her?"

"No, Nadia?" Jennifer replied.

"Name doesn't ring a bell," replied Feldman. "But if Eleni is holding her this way, she learned something about her and plans to exploit her."

Something shifted.

Not in the room.

Within Daryl.

Crystal's presence surged, not outward, but *inward*, like a tide reversing.

"Observation only," Feldman continued reading. "No surgery scheduled. No integration. Eleni flagged her personally."

"Why?" Daryl asked.

Feldman hesitated. "Because she's afraid of her."

The lights flickered.

Just once.

Jennifer felt it immediately, the hair on her arms lifting, the air tightening.

Daryl exhaled slowly. "Crystal," he said under his breath.

The blue sphere emerged near his shoulder, pulsing.

I can feel her.

Feldman stiffened. "What's happening?"

Jennifer swallowed. "I think...I think someone just discovered u in their system."

"We're not connected to them," Feldman reminded. "The data we have is downloaded."

The laptop screen glitched.

Lines of code blurred.

Then another signal appeared.

Not Helix.

Not external.

Internal.

Crystal moved closer to the screen.

She is awake.

Daryl stared. "That's not possible. Dr, Feldman said she was in a coma."

"What did she say?" asked Feldman.

Her body sleeps, her consciousness does not.

"Whoever this Sorrie Cerhess is," Daryl started, "she's awake, or at least her consciousness is!"

The room felt suddenly smaller.

Jennifer's voice was barely a whisper. "She can hear us?"

She can feel us, she has felt us since we went to Helix.

"She can feel us," started Daryl, "she became aware of us while we were at Helix."

The schematic glitched, shifted again, this time without Feldman touching the keyboard.

A new waveform appeared beside Sorrie's vitals.

Irregular.

Growing.

Feldman's eyes widened. "That's not medical telemetry."

Daryl felt it then.

A pull.

Familiar. Old. Like looking into a mirror which didn't reflect flesh.

"Crystal," he said quietly. "What is she?"

The blue light pulsed brighter.

She is convergence. Like you. Unlike you. She exists at several junctions they do not understand. She is as her name implies!

Jennifer shook her head. "Eleni keeps her asleep because she doesn't yet know how to control her without the chip implanted."

The laptop chimed softly.

A single line of text appeared at the bottom of the screen unprompted.

Please don't leave me here.

Feldman staggered back from the desk. "That...I didn't..."

Daryl was already moving.

His voice was calm. Too calm.

"We're going back."

Jennifer looked at him. "Daryl..."

"She's alone," he said. "And they're going to hurt her."

Feldman shook her head. "You barely made it out last time. They'll be ready."

Daryl turned to face them fully now.

"We can't just leave her!"

Crystal floated between them, steady and resolute.

If she remains, she will be shaped into something broken. If we lose her, we will lose everything that will ever be.

Jennifer met Daryl's eyes.

"This isn't about Helix anymore, is it?"

He shook his head once.

"No," he said. "I just learned losing her could cost us, all of us, more than we can afford to lose!"

The blue light flared.

Outside, thunder rolled faintly in the distance.

And somewhere beneath Helix Systems, a young woman waited, awake in ways no one had anticipated, and already reaching out.

EIGHTEEN

THE ELEVATOR DID not announce its arrival.

It didn't chime, didn't light up, didn't even slow perceptibly as it slid beneath Helix Systems and continued downward, past levels which previously didn't exist on any schematic Feldman had ever seen.

Eleni Kallistratos stood alone inside it, hands folded behind her back, posture flawless.

Above her, the technician's voice crackled faintly through her earpiece.

"Containment teams are active," he said. "All visible damage is being scrubbed. Survivors are being retrieved. Narratives are already seeded."

"Good," Eleni replied calmly. "Be thorough."

"Yes, Doctor."

The elevator finally slowed.

A biometric scanner slid from the wall, blue light sweeping across Eleni's eyes, then her face, then deeper, reading bone density, neural cadence, cardiac rhythm.

AUTHORIZED.

A second scan engaged at the wrist as she raised her arm without breaking stride.

PRIORITY ACCESS CONFIRMED.

The doors parted.

The air changed immediately.

Cooler. Cleaner. Sterile in a way that had nothing to do with hospitals and everything to do with control.

This was Helix's true heart.

The sublevel stretched outward in a wide, circular chamber, the ceiling lost in shadows, the walls lined with softly glowing interfaces which displayed data in constant, silent motion. There were no guards here. None were needed.

Everything and everyone that entered this place belonged to Eleni.

She walked across the polished floor, heels echoing softly, the sound swallowed almost as soon as it was made.

At the center of the chamber stood the incubation platform.

A raised dais of composite alloy and glass.

And above it—

The chamber.

It was oval, translucent, suspended in a cradle of articulated arms and humming energy fields. Fluid filled most of it, pale and faintly luminescent, threaded with diagnostic lines that pulsed in slow, steady rhythms.

Inside, floating weightless and perfectly still, was Sorrie Cerhess.

Sorrie Cerhess was twent-nine years old, but even in unconscious stillness she carried a presence which felt older, settled, resilient, quietly powerful.

She had inherited the best of both her parents. From her Haitian father came the strong, sculpted structure of her face: high cheekbones, a straight nose, and a jawline which suggested resolve rather than softness, and her secret gift. From her African American mother came warmth and depth, full lips set naturally at rest, smooth brown skin with a rich, even tone, and an expressiveness which lingered even with her eyes closed.

Her hair, thick and dark, fell in loose coils around her head, restrained only by necessity. Even unstyled, it framed her face beautifully, as if refusing to be diminished by her current state.

Sorrie's build reflected an active life, broad shoulders tapering into a strong, balanced frame, athletic without excess. There was no fragility in her posture, even now. Her body lay still, but not slack. Muscles retained a natural tension, as though some part of her remained alert beneath the induced coma, waiting.

Her hands rested loosely at her sides, fingers long and capable, unmarred by labor yet clearly accustomed to use. The faint rise and fall of her chest was steady, measured evidence of life maintained, not fading.

She looked peaceful, but not passive.

There was something about her stillness which felt deceptive, as if unconsciousness were a surface condition only, something imposed rather than accepted. The calm around her did not feel like surrender. It felt like suspension.

As though whatever made Sorrie Cerhess special had not gone quiet at all.

Only silent.

Her body was untouched. No incisions. No implants yet.

Barely breathing.

Induced coma.

Alive.

Eleni stopped a few feet from the chamber and tilted her head, studying the young woman as one might examine a rare artifact.

"So," she said softly, her voice carrying easily in the quiet space. This is you."

The chamber responded with a subtle shift in light, systems acknowledging her presence.

Eleni stepped closer.

"You've been... expensive," she continued conversationally. "Time, resources, discretion. All for someone who hasn't even shown her hand yet."

She smiled faintly.

"Oh sure there are rumors of the young woman who helped the boy who also happens to be a dragon, but no solid proof of him or you. But that's always how it begins, isn't it? Rumors, conjecture, yadda yadda."

Her fingers brushed the glass, just once.

"I knew something was wrong the moment I felt the interference," Eleni went on. "Linard was an anomaly. Harding was... an inconvenience."

Her eyes narrowed slightly as she looked at Sorrie's face.

"But *you*," she murmured. "You were hidden, for a while."

A pause.

"You're not like them," Eleni said. "Not...not bound by the same... limitations."

She straightened, hands clasped behind her back once more.

"You don't announce yourself," she continued. "You play behind the scenes. You *listen*. You wait. You survive and yet, somehow, we still found you!"

The monitors around the chamber flickered briefly, reacting to a subtle spike in neural activity.

Eleni noticed.

Of course she did.

"There it is," she said, pleased. "That's the question, isn't it? What exactly are you?"

She circled the chamber slowly.

"Yes, Helix makes soldiers," Eleni started. "That's the truth. We make *alignment*. Purpose. Order."

She stopped directly in front of Sorrie again.

"And you, my dear, are going to be magnificent."

Her voice lowered, almost intimate.

"Once I understand you... once I unlock what makes you special, learn of all of your connections... you won't need to be controlled."

She smiled, this time without warmth.

"You'll *want* to serve."

Eleni turned away from the chamber, already finished with the moment.

"Prepare the adaptive suite," she said calmly into her comm. "And double the isolation parameters. No external interfaces."

A beat.

"And make sure she's comfortable."

The chamber hummed softly, lights stabilizing.

Behind her, Sorrie remained still.

But somewhere deep within the fluid and silence, Sorrie was listening.

She will remember.

NINETEEN

JENNIFER STOOD BY the bathroom window, phone pressed to her ear, the hum of the hotel's air unit the only thing keeping the silence from collapsing in on her.

"Dad?"

There was a pause on the other end. Not static. Breath.

She paused while listening.

"I..." She swallowed. "I'm sorry. Things have been...complicated."

Another pause. Longer this time.

Something she heard over the phone changed her expression immediately.

"When?" Jennifer asked.

Jennifer closed her eyes. A tear descended the left side of her cheek as the bathroom light flickered faintly above her, reacting to something she didn't consciously direct.

"I should have known," she whispered. "I should have been there."

Tears burned at the corners of her eyes, but she didn't let them fall.

"Are Tommy and Michelle there?" she asked as she sniffled.

Another pause.

"I'm coming," Jennifer said. "I'll be there tonight."

A long pause as she closed her eyes and sobbed quietly.

"I love you dad!"

She ended the call and stood there for a long moment, phone still in her hand, shoulders tight.

When she stepped back into the room, Daryl looked up immediately.

"You okay Jennifer?"

She didn't try to soften it. "My mom's in the hospital. She had a stroke."

Feldman's expression shifted instantly, sympathy, concern, understanding all crossing her face at once.

"Oh Elaine," she said empathetically.

For a brief moment, Jennifer forgot Dr. Feldman knew her parents. "I need to go," Jennifer said. "My parents need me."

Daryl nodded. No hesitation. No resentment.

"You should," he said simply.

Jennifer looked at him, conflict flashing across her face. "Sorrie?"

"I've got her," Daryl said.

Something in his voice made Feldman look up sharply.

"Daryl," she said carefully, "you don't mean alone."

He met her gaze. "I mean...I got her...and I'm not alone he said as the spherical blue orb emanated from his torso."

Feldman exhaled slowly and turned back to the laptop. "Then you'll need this."

She pulled up the schematics again, fingers moving with renewed urgency.

"They moved her," Feldman said. "Deeper. Sublevel four. Isolated power grid. Manual security redundancies."

Daryl leaned over her shoulder, absorbing everything.

"They expect an army," Feldman continued. "They don't expect someone who doesn't care if he comes back."

Jennifer's chest tightened. "Daryl..."

He turned to her.

"I know the risk," he said calmly. "And I know what happens to her if I don't go."

Jennifer stepped closer, placing a hand on Daryl's arm.

"Don't die," she said quietly.

He gave her the smallest smile. "I'll try not to."

Feldman looked between them, then nodded once.

"I'll stay here," she said. "Keep an eye on your parents."

Daryl nodded his appreciation.

Jennifer took a breath, steadying herself.

"I'll come back," she said as she grabbed her things and headed to the door. "As soon as I can."

Daryl watched her go, watched the door close behind her, and then turned back to the screen.

"Show me the fastest way in," he said.

"You wanna write this down?" She asked.

"No need," he said. "I have an eidetic memory."

There was no darkness.

That was the first thing Sorrie noticed.

People always talked about how comas were like moments of sleep, like sinking into black water. But this wasn't that. It was more like standing in a place where the lights had been left on, but the walls were all missing.

She couldn't feel her body.

No weight. No pain. No breath.

Just awareness.

She tried to move, and the idea of movement echoed back at her like a question which hadn't been answered yet.

Hello? she thought, unsure if thinking still worked.

Nothing answered.

She reached outward, not with words, not with sound, but with the same instinct she'd had her whole life, the one which made her feel like she was always just a step out of sync with the world.

Her sister April had called it her *spacing out face.*

Jade?

Gemini?

Snake?

The names she called out to surfaced without effort, familiar in a way she couldn't explain as her memory was a bit skewed in this state. She pushed toward them; toward whatever thread she thought connected her to the others and hit a wall.

Not resistance.

Absence.

They weren't there.

A flicker of panic rose in her chest, or where her chest should have been.

Why can't I reach you?

Because you are not Nelarian.

The voice didn't come from anywhere.

It came *with* her.

Sorrie startled, not physically, but in the way thoughts scatter when you realize you're not alone in your own head.

Who are you?

A pause.

Then, gently:

I am Crystal.

The name felt...warm. Familiar. Like hearing a song you didn't know you remembered.

Are you real? Sorrie asked.

As real as you are right now, Crystal replied.

Sorrie hesitated. *Am I dead?*

Crystal chuckled. *Everyone always asks that, but no.*

That answer was immediate. Certain.

You are resting between moments.

Sorrie considered that. It felt right in a way nothing else had since she'd been brought here.

They're keeping me asleep, she said. It wasn't a question.

Yes.

Why?

Because they are afraid of you and most people are afraid of what they don't understand.

But that's not all.

They intend to weaponize you once they know your secrets.

That scared her more than she expected.

I don't want to hurt anyone, Sorrie said quickly. *I just want to go home.*

You will, Crystal said. *Help is already moving toward you.*

Sorrie clung to that. *Who?*

Someone who remembers what it means to choose.

The space around her shifted, not visually, but emotionally, and suddenly another thought pressed forward, sharp and aching.

April, Sorrie said.

The name hurt.

My sister... she died. But sometimes it feels like she didn't. Like something stopped halfway.

Crystal was quiet for a long time.

Then:

Yes.

Sorrie's awareness came alive. *You know what happened to her.*

I do.

She changed, Sorrie said. *Before she died. I felt it. Something was wrong.*

Crystal's presence softened.

If she had been allowed to continue, Crystal said, her body would have been reshaped into something that was not truly her.

Sorrie recoiled. *You stopped it.*

Yes.

Why?

Because April Jenkins was not meant to be lost that way.

Sorrie swallowed, though she had no throat. *Jade helped her later. He brought her memories back.*

Yes, Crystal said. *He did what he could within time.*

And you? Sorrie asked. *What did you do?*

I made sure she stayed with her body so that she could still be found.

That answer lingered.

Sorrie felt something click into place, not understanding, exactly, but acceptance.

We're connected, she said.

Crystal's presence brightened, *just a little.*

You do not know it yet, Crystal said, *but we have been friends for a very long time.*

Sorrie frowned. *That doesn't make sense. I'm twent-nine.*

Time does not move the way you think it does.

Sorrie let that settle.

Am I going to wake up?

Yes.

When?

When it is safe.

A beat.

And then, softly:

He is coming.

Sorrie felt it then, a distant pull, steady and determined, like a signal cutting through fog.

Tell him thank you, she said.

Crystal's reply carried something like a smile.

You can tell him yourself.

The space around Sorrie warmed.

And for the first time since the machines had put her to sleep, she wasn't afraid anymore.

TWENTY

THE NIGHT AROUND Helix Systems was unnaturally still.

There were no sirens. There were no alarms. There was no movement.

For Daryl that was the tell.

He once again leapt over the fence and stood on the edge of the compound, rain-dark jacket phased into his black biker outfit with helmet in place, the blue seams dimmed to near invisibility.

"They're expecting chaos," Lazer Droid murmured. "Not silence."

Correct, their predictive models are calibrated for force.

"Then let's disappoint them."

He moved.

No sprint. No dramatic leap. Just forward, slipping between blind spots, cameras going dark a half second before he crossed their range.

As cameras moved to catch a glimpse, Crystal would throw up a blue shield which would loop a quiet and clear field of vision for anyone watching.

Engaging the chaotic light optical altercation kernel mechanism.

"Really? You could've just said cloaking mechanism."

Doors unlocked themselves with soft clicks, not breaches.

Inside, Helix breathed.

Servers hummed. Lights glowed. The building felt awake in a way that made his skin crawl, like something pretending to be alive.

Two guards stood at the first checkpoint.

They never saw him.

Lazer Droid stepped in behind the first, applying pressure with surgical precision.

The woman went slack without a sound.

The second guard, a man, turned just in time to register confusion before a controlled strike shut him down.

"No permanent damage," Lazer Droid whispered. "Whether they choose this or not."

Vital signs are stable, no serious injuries.

They approached an elevator.

"This is the one from the schematic Dr. Feldman showed us, "he said confidently.

Affirmative.

"Access and take over the system..."

The golf ball sized laser light interrupted Lazer Droid as it moved forward and into the access panel for the system.

The door to the elevator soon opened.

Already done.

He stepped into the elevator. "Look at you being proactive!"

The doors closed.

He descended.

The elevator first reached sublevel one.

Sublevel two.

The air grew colder, drier. The walls thicker.

The elevator stopped as sublevel three required manual access.

The blue light moved into the system and Crystal looped through the lock, rewriting authorization in real time.

Then a chime.

Sublevel four.

The doors slid open and Lazer Droid walked out slowly and deliberately.

"This is almost too easy Crystal."

Talk about ease of the mission when you're back at the hotel.

"You've got a point."

The corridor was different here. No signage. No color. Just reinforced walls and recessed lighting which felt more like observation than illumination.

"She's close," Daryl said.

He felt her now, not as a signal, but as a presence. Steady. Waiting.

At the end of the corridor stood a single door.

No markings.

No windows.

A biometric lock pulsed faintly.

Crystal moved ahead of him, light threading through the interface like a needle.

Containment ward identified. Subject stable. Consciousness active.

Lazer Droid looked around at the rim of the door.

"Hang on Sorrie," he said. "I'm here."

The door slid open.

Inside, the room was small too small. One incubation chamber. One console. Tubes and monitors which whispered numbers meant to keep a body obedient.

Next to the chamber sat a table with what looked like a backpack.

Sorrie Cerhess lay at the center of it all.

She looked peaceful.

Her chest rose and fell slowly, deliberately, as if even breathing had been negotiated.

Without uttering a word, Lazer Droid directed Crystal to the backpack.

She moved through the back briefly, scanning all contents.

The blue orb soon resurfaced. *This pack seems to be important.*

"Anything that can act as a tracker?"

Negative.

Lazer Droid placed the backpack over his right shoulder and then crossed the room without hesitation to the top of the chamber. He placed his hand gently on the side of the incubation chamber.

The monitors spiked.

Not dangerously, recognizably.

She knows you're here!

"Scan for injuries!"

Crytal scanned her blue light over the length of Sorrie's body.

All previously mentioned fractures have healed.

"Great," he started, "that will make this next part easier. Scan all vitals, homeostatic patterns, and biological D-N-A, duplicate and be prepared to replace a corporal image data set in the system...loop it for eighteen minutes!"

On it.

Crystal did as Lazer Droid requested and a blue digital ghost copy of Sorrie appeared positioned over her body and lowered into her exact current position.

T minus eighteen minutes!

He moved to the console and began disconnecting lines — carefully, methodically. Each tube removed sent a tremor through the system, alarms flashing briefly then quick and quiet suppression.

"Easy," Daryl murmured as he lifted the heavily sedated woman out of the chamber. "I've got you."

He slid one arm beneath Sorrie's shoulders and another under her knees, lifting her effortlessly. The moment her body left the bed, the machine protested with a red light which beeped once.

Crystal surged, blue light flooding the console.

Adjusting for weight counterbalance. System override complete.

The room fell quiet.

Sorrie stirred.

Not awake but beginning to get there.

Lazer Droid adjusted his grip and turned toward the door.

That's when the corridor lights snapped on all at once.

Footsteps echoed.

Not running.

Approaching.

"They're coming," Lazer Droid said calmly.

Yes, but they are too late. Engaging reflective shield.

Lazer Droid appeared to have become invisible.

The guards moved passed him and he passed them.

He stepped back into the elevator carrying Sorrie like something sacred, his presence bending the air just enough to keep cameras blind and sensors confused.

Now that's a cloaking device added Crystal.

As he moved, one thought anchored him completely:

This ends now.

Behind him, Helix Systems realized it had lost something it would never fully understand.

And somewhere between moments, Sorrie felt herself being carried toward waking.

TWENTY-ONE

ELENI KALLISTRATOS DIDN'T raise her voice. That wasn't her way.

That was part of what made her unsettling.

The secure sublevel of Helix Systems was immaculate, white floors unmarred by blood, lights humming at a frequency calibrated to calm the nervous system. The technicians now stationed there due to the apparent break in of a ghost who managed to by-pass all of Helix's protocols, sat perfectly still, eyes fixed on their consoles, hands hovering uselessly over keyboards.

The incubation chamber sat empty and alone.

Eleni stared at it.

"Say it again," she said quietly.

The technician swallowed. "The subject was removed, ma'am. Systems show an unforced disengagement of the chamber locks followed by a complete sensor blackout. No fatalities. No residual energy signatures we could trace."

Eleni stepped closer to the glass, resting two fingers against its surface.

"That chamber was shielded," she said. "Redundant. Buried beneath layers of security I designed myself."

"Yes, ma'am."

"And yet," she continued, voice tightening just a fraction, "she's gone?"

The technician nodded, sweat beading at his temple. "Her vitals and homeostatic patterns continued to show up on our displays for at least ten minutes after we realized she was gone."

Eleni turned slowly, her eyes sharp now, burning. "Do you know how many contingencies existed for that girl?"

"No, ma'am."

"Neither did anyone else," Eleni replied. "Which was the point. There's no way that anything should've been bypassed!"

She looked down and exhaled, long, slow and measured, and then reached up and pressed her palm flat against the wall console.

Screens bloomed to life around her, surveillance footage, biometric logs, predictive models fracturing and reforming in real time.

"They didn't just take her," she said. "They *understood* her."

Her jaw clenched.

"That means Feldman knew more than I gave her credit for, Linard and Harding are far more capable than projected. Their existence is no longer intriguing, it's problematic!"

The technician dared to speak. "Orders, Dr. Kallistratos?"

Eleni straightened, composure snapping back into place like armor sealing shut.

"I'm going to need a suitable candidate...since my agents are all free thinkers now, I want an absolute loyalist who will be willing to get systemic upgrades and weapons added in order to do what I need."

"We don't have weapons we can add to our current systems?" queried the technician.

"We have purchased patents from Biotech when they overhauled their research division a few years back," she corrected. "Find me a volunteer!"

She paused.

"Destiny doesn't make mistakes," Eleni added softly. "But it does make enemies."

***

The hotel room smelled faintly of Lipton black tea.

Sorrie sat cross-legged on the edge of the bed, a thin blanket wrapped around her shoulders, her dark curls still damp from the shower Feldman had insisted on.

She looked calm, awake, alert, but her eyes carried a weight which hadn't been there before Helix.

Dr. Nadia Feldman snapped her gloves off and dropped them into the trash. "Vitals are stable," she said. "No signs of neural intrusion. Whatever they were planning, they hadn't started it yet."

"That's good," Sorrie said quietly. "I think."

The door to the room clicked open.

Daryl stepped in carrying two paper bags and a cardboard tray of drinks. "Alright," he announced, "I got lo mein, dumplings, something spicy I don't recognize, and three forks because apparently I'm an optimist."

Sorrie blinked. Then laughed a short, surprised sound which seemed to catch her off guard.

"Thank you," she said.

Daryl nodded as he set the bags down. "Figured after being kidnapped by a megacorp and induced in a coma, you earned carbs."

Feldman watched Sorrie carefully as she sat down across from her. "Sorrie," she said gently, "do you have any idea why Helix would want you specifically?"

Sorrie hesitated.

Then she nodded.

"My father," she said. "He was a practitioner. Haitian lineage. Old magic. He never called it sorcery, but that's what it was." She looked down at her hands. "He said it wasn't something you learn, it's something that wakes up."

"And yours did," Feldman said.

"He died when I was a child and returned to tell me of my destiny," Sorrie replied. "Over the years since that time, I could feel patterns, foresee future events, cast spells. Subtly. Under the radar." She swallowed. "I think Helix noticed because I recently helped someone using a lot of magic."

"You can see the future but had no idea they were coming for you?" Daryl asked.

"My gift doesn't quite work that way," started Sorrie, "What I see are the events that require my intervention."

"So you think you were supposed to be there," asked Feldman. "Why?"

"Not sure as of yet," she replied, "but I will learn in time. I like to know things, cause I'm a planner. I believe if you fail to plan, then you plan to fail!"

Daryl looked at her and then at Dr. Feldman, and chuckled.

"What?" asked Feldman.

"The story I told you and Jennifer about my past," Daryl remembered fondly, "That was something Crystal always said to me."

"I'm afraid though, that my rescue is going to send this Eleni down a different path."

Daryl frowned. "They've been building an army," he said. "Bionic limbs. Neural control chips. They started with people who needed help...then went looking for people who didn't. They made soldiers who didn't know they were soldiers."

Feldman nodded. "We've destroyed the neural control chip for the soldiers they have already amassed, but I am sure they will create another. Now they're also branching out to people who will be satisfied with what can be given to them."

"Or what they can get from them now," Sorrie said softly. "They were planning to give me limbs I didn't need. Thank you all!"

Daryl met her gaze. "No problem."

Sorrie looked between them, then straightened. "If Eleni wanted me," she said, "it's because she thinks I can help her control the ones she *can't*."

Silence settled over the room.

Outside, a car passed on the highway, tires hissing against wet pavement.

Feldman finally spoke. "Then she's going to keep coming."

Daryl leaned back in his chair, arms folding. "Good," he said. "Because now we know what she's really after."

Sorrie nodded slowly.

"So do I."

TWENTY-TWO

THE ROOM HAD no windows. It could've been used as an interrogation room but there was no bidirectional window nor was there a mirror in the room indicating that someone could watch during the session.

She had it designed that way intentionally.

The camera was hidden in the wall as was the microphone in the event she ever needed to listen to a conversation taking place in the room or if she ever needed to revisit a previous conversation she had, if only to solidify the details of her own memory.

Her design in other words was intentional.

The man seated at the center of the table sat perfectly still, back straight, hands resting calmly on the reinforced armrests. From the waist down, he was all Helix, two silver prosthetic legs from the hip down, humming softly with power.

Major Thomas Reddy, Former U.S. Army. Now retired.

He was a combat engineer. He completed two tours in Afghanistan. An IED just outside of Kandahar had taken both his legs and half his squad.

Helix had given him back his life and even though he was initially unaware of the life of servitude for which was imposed upon him, He had an improved life, better than before he had even enlisted. His became the kind of loyalty, money couldn't buy.

Dr. Eleni Kallistratos circled him slowly, heels clicking softly against the polished floor.

"Last time we performed the surgery, you adapted faster than projected," she said.

"Yes maam," answered Reddy.

"No need for formality Red," started Eleni as she stopped in front of him, still standing and looking down at him. "I can call you Red?"

"Sure can Maam...Eleni," he corrected. "They used to call me Red when I served 'cause I had a tendency to always make my enemies bleed!"

A little on the nose she thought but she liked his candor.

Eleni started walking again as his eyes followed. "Even after the command layer was disrupted, you stayed with Helix. Why?"

Red's body tightened. "I didn't need to be controlled," he replied. "Helix gave me purpose. Gave me *movement*."

Eleni stopped in front of him and met his eyes. "And loyalty?"

"You'll never have ta question mine," he said without hesitation.

That was the answer she wanted.

A gesture, and the wall behind her came alive, schematics unfolding in luminous layers. Prosthetic arm with upgrades, super-upgrades. Reinforced spine. Ocular targeting systems. Integrated weapons platforms nested so seamlessly they looked like anatomy rather than machinery.

Reds leaned forward, awe flickering across his face.

"Ain't much wrong with my arms!"

"Can you punch through two inches of solid steel?"

"You'd make me more than I was," he said quietly.

Eleni smiled. "I would make you *complete*."

She let the moment settle before continuing.

"Retrograde self-cooling rocket boosters on the outside of your back, with a sub-posterior lower back plating that keeps you from feeling the heat from your jet pack. Your eyes out fitted with telescopic targeting guidance systems, linked into your neuronal circuitry which will allow for smooth targeting even when distracted in a fight. You will also be able to analyze fight patterns to quickly grab the upper hand."

"These aren't rinky dink upgrades Eleni, and without you sharing the specifics, they look like they are worth a pretty penny. So, who I got to kill?"

"There are three individuals threatening Helix," she said. "Daryl Linard, Jennifer Harding, and Nadia Feldman." She slid a folder over to him and he opened it.

The first picture he saw was Linard's, in regular clothes and then in his gear as Lazer Droid."

"What's the 'L-D' on the chest for?"

"Little Dick? Who cares? He's your primary target."

"I hope this doesn't turn into somethin' racial," started Red as he looked up from the picture. "You know çause I'm white and he's black."

Eleni thought briefly about changing her mind.

"That's your biggest concern?" She then spread out the other photos. "Don't worry, he's always wearing that stupid helmet when he's fighting and the two ladies are white, well, one's Jewish, but you get the point."

Red looked down at the other pictures, and he picked up the picture of Jennifer. "She's a looker," he said.

"You best not mess with that one, she can shock your privates!"

He dropped her photo.

"She might be a little harder, you'll have to sneak attack her," started Eleni, "Her powers deal with electricity and magnetism so if she gets her sights on you, it could be game over being that your prosthetics respond to electrical impulses from your neuro chip."

"What about the last one?" Red asked. "What's her super power?"

"She's super annoying and a nuisance."

Red's expression hardened. "Say no more, I'm in, especially if you get me these upgrades!"

Eleni smiled.

"They've taken something from us, and I intend to take *everything* from them."

Red nodded once. "Understood!"

Behind her calm exterior, Eleni noted the moment, his eagerness, his certainty.

And she silently authorized the hidden update to his neuro chip.

The update he would never know about.

* * *

Outside of The Monongahela Crest Hotel, in the parking lot, Daryl stood outside of the Honda Accord rental car and smiled at Sorrie who was sitting in the driver's seat with the car running.

Dr. Feldman stood next to him smiling.

He passed some papers to her.

"Once you get to Philadelphia," Daryl started, "you have a couple of days to take this to the Enterprise on Cheltenham Avenue, a few blocks off of Broad Street, I believe that's the closest one to where you live. Please call when you make it back."

"Daryl, I don't know how to emphasize how thankful I am for your help," started Sorrie, "all three of you! And thanks again for grabbing my stuff!"

"That was Crystal!" exclaimed Daryl.

Feldman chuckled.

"Thank you Crystal," Sorrie said excitedly'

My pleasure, us girls have to stick together!

"She said..."

"My pleasure, us girls have to stick together," interrupted Sorrie. "

"You can hear her?" asked Daryl as Feldman looked at him with surprise and then back at Sorrie.

"Didn't she tell you? We go way back," she said as she pulled out of the parking space. "She then pulled off."

"Way back?" asked Feldman. "She's only twenty-nine?"

That's what Sorrie said to me.

Daryl chuckled.

"So you ready for the Airport?"

"As ready as I'll ever be," started Feldman, "cab should be here any minute!"

"Thank you for your help," smiled Daryl, "we couldn't have done all the good we did if you hadn't helped us!"

"You were both pretty convincing. I should be thanking you, both of you! Please give my warmest to Jennifer!"

Daryl nodded as a cab soon pulled up. "Crystal cleared all info on you so you should be good flying over there!"

Dr. Feldman kissed Daryl on the cheek. "You take care of yourself; I worry that Eleni will retaliate against you."

"There's a thirty-five percent probability that she will retaliate," Daryl said.

"That's the percentage I'm worried about!" Feldman then got in the cab and Daryl closed the door for her.

The cab then sped off.

TWENTY-THREE

DARYL STROLLED INTO the living room where his parents were sitting around watching television and he plopped down onto the couch.

"I bet you miss Baltimore now son," said Henry.

"The probability of you winning said bet is at hundred percent if I took it," replied Daryl.

"Yeah I'm still not fond of that."

Patrice laughed. "Oh Hank, we got our baby back, don't ruin movie night!"

Shadow moved over closer to Daryl as he started munching on the popcorn.

"You know I don't mean nothing by it," said Henry.

Henry aimed the remote and changed the channel to Channel four and the news was on.

"Son I forgot to pop the DVD in, do you mind?"

Daryl rose from his seat, "not at all, where is it?" He looked around.

The first news report came across the television.

—*explosions reported at Riverfront Commons Mall. Multiple casualties. Witnesses describe a single attacker moving with mechanical precision*—

Patrice Linard's hand flew to her mouth.

Henry leaned forward, eyes narrowing. "That's not—"

The screen cut to shaky footage.

A man standing in the center of the atrium.

A lone I.C.E. agent walking with a semi-automatic weapon as local law enforcement orders him to stand down and start shooting at him. Security teams scattered like leaves.

Patrice whispered, "Dear God...when is it ever going to stop?"

Daryl started for the door.

"Son are we ever going to be finished with them?" asked Henry.

"I hope to answer that question today!"

"Be careful son," said Patrice.

"I promise mom!" Daryl then left out the door.

He hopped on his motorcycle and took off, immediately heading for the expressway.

As he pulled the bike onto the expressway, his clothing phased into his all-black leather gear, helmet changing slightly in configuration as the blue light traced over him and the seams of his suit and over the bike, changing him into Lazer Droid as he raced through the e-way.

"He has to be some sort of Helix loyalist, a true I.C.E. agent," he muttered. "Looks to be without fear."

Probability of confrontation exceeds acceptable thresholds. Daryl...he is bait.

"I know," Daryl replied racing the bike. "But there are innocent people in the area. Helix keeps drawing a new line to cross!"

***

The mall was chaos.

Glass shattered. Smoke hung thick in the air. And at the center of it all, Red, dressed in all black fatigues, face covering hiding just his nose and the lower half of his face.

He continued to fire his weapon into the air in various directions.

He laughed maniacally. "Come on little biker boy or electric girl, where are you?" he asked out loud but to himself.

He soon heard the unmistakable distant sound of the buzz of a motorcycle getting faster and closer.

Red turned to his left and spied Lazer Droid moving fast towards him. He dropped his weapons and started running towards him.

As they moved within yards of each other Lazer Droid flew off the bike as Red leapt up towards him.

They collided like freight trains.

Red was stronger and threw the first strike which landed on the left side of Lazer Droids face with the weight of Helix engineering behind it.

Lazer Droid was thrown through storefronts until he crashed into a wall and fell to the floor.

Red immediately ran in after him. and pinned each arm down with his bilateral neuro titanium legs.

Lazer Droid grunted painfully.

Red threw blows at each side of Lazer Droids helmet and after several blows, it started to crack on each side.

Lazer Droid lay stuck, pinned, crushed beneath blows meant to end him.

"This ends today," Red said as he stepped off of Lazer Droid's arms and grabbed him by the throat. "Your death means Helix *survives*."

Lazer Droids' body screamed warnings within him as the majority of his face shielding fell off.

Structural integrity failing.

Then once I finish with you, I will visit both of your girlfriends, first the young one, and then...the older one!"

Then something snapped into place.

Not rage.

Resolve.

"You're fighting on a leash," Lazer Droid said hoarsely. "I'm fighting for *everyone's free will! Including yours*."

"My will is free," rasped Red. "I appreciate Helix, and I choose to kill the three of you willingly."

The blue light surged, not outward, but inward. Reinforcing.

Red threw another punch directly at Lazer Droids face and sent the android flying back several hundred feet where he crashed into another wall.

Red again moved towards him. "See you are just a man, man dies, I have upgrades, the kind you can only dream of having! When everything is complete, I will be everything that you're not!"

The rocket boosters exited his back and Red flew upward and looked down in the area where Lazer Droid fell.

Lazer Droid stood up as the blue laser light quickly went to work on restoring his helmet and fixing his injuries as Red looked on with disbelief.

The light then dissipated as it repaired the helmet, restoring the full-face shield. "Your right, man does die, but I am not just a man, I'm a Lazer Droid!" He then leapt up and into Red, tackled him at the waist, and brought him down to the ground.

The fight turned.

Red swung again, harder this time, but Lazer Droid didn't retreat.

He blocked, redirected attempted contacts, and stepped into it.

A swift blow from Red glanced off his shoulder as Lazer Droid drove a knee upward, cracking against Red's reinforced abdomen.

The impact boomed through the night air like a wrecking ball.

Red staggered back a step; surprise flashed across his face for the first time.

"You can adapt," Red snarled. "Well biker boy, so can I!"

Hydraulic pressure screamed as Red's prosthetic legs locked, pistons firing.

He lunged forward, arms transforming mid-stride, plating shifted, ports opened, blades slid free from beneath the bilateral upper silver appendages.

Lazer Droid caught the first strike from the right barehanded.

Metal shrieked as his grip tightened around Red's wrist. The blade bent. And then snapped.

Red Screamed.

"I thought pain receptors were blocked," started Lazer Droid.

Crystal scanned quickly. *They are, it's psychosomatic. It looks like it should hurt to his eyes so in his mind...*

"It does!" interrupted Lazer Droid. "Since it doesn't really hurt, I can now bring the pain!"

Red roared and swung with the other arm.

Lazer Droid ducked low, swept Red's leg out from under him, then gripped upward, grabbing a hold of his other prosthetic arm and tearing the left prosthetic clean from its socket in a shower of sparks and hydraulic fluid.

Red hit the ground screaming.

Not from pain.

From loss.

"NO!" Red bellowed, scrambling with his remaining limbs. "You don't get to take this from me!"

"I'm not," Lazer Droid said, voice cold, controlled. "Helix is taking this away from you, since YOU chose to fight."

Red fired point-blank from a weapon port embedded in his shoulder.

Lazer Droid twisted aside as the blast scorched past him, then surged forward, slamming his fist into Red's chest hard enough to crater the armor beneath.

Red coughed, systems stuttering.

Lazer Droid moved faster now, precise, surgical.

He grabbed Red's remaining leg at the knee joint and twisted as Red Screamed.

The prosthetic tore loose with a thunderous crack, severed cleanly at the coupling. Red collapsed, thrashing, trying to drag himself forward with his right arm.

Still dangerous.

Still reaching.

Red triggered his last upgrade.

His right arm locked into combat configuration, plating sealing, internal weapons powering up. He ignited his jet pack and flew up wildly, swung forcefully in desperation replacing discipline.

Lazer Droid caught his forearm mid-strike, stopping him.

"I won't kill you," Lazer Droid said quietly, leaning in close so Red could hear him over the alarms screaming in his body. "But I *will* end this."

He wrenched one arm free and drove his elbow down at the joint, *once*.

The limb tore away.

Red screamed.

Lazer Droid didn't stop.

He turned, braced, and pulled the remaining leg free with a violent twist, the sound echoing like tearing steel cables.

Red collapsed fully now.

No functional limbs.

No weapons.

No upgrades except for the useless jetpack and telescopic eyes.

Just a man, screaming in horror, trapped inside the wreckage Helix had made of him.

Lazer Droid stood over him, chest heaving, blue light flickering along his frame.

"You wanted me broken," he said. "Now you know what that feels like."

Red sobbed, rage gone, loyalty shattered into nothing but terror.

Eleni will continue. As long as Helix exists.

Lazer Droid looked at the burning mall, the terrified faces, the damage left behind.

"Then we stop playing cat and mouse. We cut her off at the source, once and for all," he said.

He turned away and started walking as his bike soon pulled up alongside of him. He mounted the bike as more sirens closed in.

"I'm taking Helix off the board," he said. "And after that..."

The engine roared.

"...we hunt who's left."

I'm with you til the end, said Crystal.

They then took off towards the expressway.

TWENTY-FOUR

HELIX SYSTEMS DIDN'T scream when Lazer Droid returned.

The compound rose from the industrial outskirts like it always had, polished, confident, unnatural in how clean it looked beneath a moonless sky.

The glass façade reflected the dim highway lights and the low clouds passing overhead, as if the building itself was pretending to be nothing more than an expensive corporate headquarters

There was no lock down. There was no howling of alarms or flood of troops within its halls.

The building was just, quiet.

Lazer Droid stood at the edge of the perimeter fence, helmet on, hands relaxed at his sides. Blue laser lights on his seems and reflecting off his trusty bike at his side.

No patrols.

No I.C.E. silhouettes cutting across the upper windows.

No movement at all.

"Too quiet," he muttered. "Crytal activate the chaotic light optical altercation engine on the bike please!"

Oh you want me to Cloak the bike?

Lazer Droid laughed. "Now you're learning."

The silence ahead indicates evacuation protocols initiated. Probability: seventy eight percent.

"Or a trap," Lazer Droid replied.

He moved anyway.

The fence didn't stop him. It never really had. He vaulted it with ease and landed silently on the other side.

The air smelled like damp pavement, cold steel, and something faintly electrical, like the aftertaste of lightning.

He crossed the courtyard toward the service entrance.

The door should've been locked.

It wasn't.

Lazer Droid paused with his hand on the bar.

He didn't like it.

Then he pushed inside.

***

The interior was colder than the night outside.

Helix always ran its halls the same way, temperature controlled, air filtered, sterile enough to feel like a lab even when you were only passing office doors.

But now the building had a different kind of cold.

The cold of a place which had been abandoned too quickly.

An open security kiosk sat empty. A half-finished cup of coffee had congealed into darkness. A jacket hung on the back of a chair like someone had stood up and never sat down again.

Lazer Droid walked past them.

His boots made no sound.

Emergency floor lighting had activated in thin amber strips along the baseboards. It cast everything in a low glow which made corners feel deeper than they should've been.

He didn't look at the cameras tracking him.

But he *felt* them.

"Crystal," he started under his breath. "Are they watching?"

Active lenses are cycling in standby mode. Network coverage degraded. Observation possible. Broadcast capability disabled.

"Good," Lazer Droid started. "Then no one stops what happens next."

He moved deeper into the building.

***

He had already placed two charges in the lower level, structural supports, not flashy points. Not a fireball, not an explosion meant for the news.

127

A collapse.

A clean erasure.

Helix didn't deserve a spectacle.

It deserved to be removed.

As he walked, Lazer Droid pulled a small device from his pocket, simple, black, unmarked. He pressed it gently to the wall at a junction where metal met reinforced concrete.

A soft click.

Magnetic clamp engaged.

A thin blue ring pulsed once, confirmation.

Lazer Droid stepped back and watched it for a second longer than necessary.

Not because he feared failure.

Because he wanted the moment to register.

"This ends," he whispered, assuring himself.

He turned and continued upward.

***

The stairwell echoed, empty and hollow.

Level after level.

The higher he climbed, the more it felt like he was entering a place which didn't belong to the world outside.

Corporate offices became more private.

Security doors became thicker.

Keypads became biometric.

Lazer Droid never slowed his pace.

On the ninth floor, he found a hallway lined with framed patents and polished awards, Helix's trophies displayed like religious relics.

On the tenth floor, the lights were out completely.

Only the glow of city spilled-through and lit the glass walls faintly.

Lazer Droid stepped into the darkness.

Then he stopped.

A light was on at the far end.

Just one.

A single office with the door half-closed.

It shouldn't have been lit.
It shouldn't have been occupied.
Lazer Droid's hand lifted instinctively.
A blue shimmer crawled over his knuckles.
He moved forward.
Slowly.

TWENTY-FIVE

HE PUSHED THE office door open.

And for the first time since he'd entered Helix, the silence broke.

Not with an alarm.

With a voice.

Low. Controlled. Calm.

"You came back."

Eleni Kallistratos stood behind the desk.

Not seated.

Standing.

As if she'd been waiting for someone who wasn't supposed to arrive.

She wasn't in a lab coat. She wasn't in heels. She wore a fitted black outfit that looked more like a uniform than fashion, clean lines, no jewelry, hair pulled back tight.

Her eyes were sharp.

But there was something else in them too.

Surprise.

Real surprise.

Lazer Droid didn't move.

His visor reflected her office, dim lighting, a wall of screens, the city skyline beyond the glass.

"I half expected you," she continued. "I should have known since you defeated Major Red, you would make your way back here."

"You're still here?" he said with a twinge of surprise in his words.

Eleni exhaled slowly, almost amused.

"I didn't expect you to be so calm," she replied. "I expected you to be angry."

"I'm both," Lazer Droid said.

She tilted her head slightly. "Where's Harding?"

"Not here," Lazer Droid said.

"And Feldman?"

"Also not here!"

Eleni smiled faintly. "So you did keep her."

Lazer Droid stepped in fully, closing the door behind him.

The click sounded loud in the quiet office.

Eleni's eyes flicked to the door.

Then back to him.

Then, just for a split second, to the hallway beyond.

As if she suddenly realized something.

As if she suddenly wondered why he would close a door in a building he believed empty.

"Your security teams are gone," Lazer Droid said. "Your I.C.E. network is fractured. Your facility is..."

"Compromised," Eleni finished calmly, "yes. I'm well aware."

"Then why are you still here?"

Eleni stepped out from behind the desk.

Her voice stayed smooth, but her body had shifted, subtle readiness.

"I wanted to see you," she said. "Up close."

Lazer Droid took another step forward.

The distance between them shrank.

Eleni didn't flinch.

"You're not just an escaped asset," she continued. "You're an anomaly. Something outside the architecture."

Lazer Droid's tone stayed even. "I am different. I'm not quite what I was, you changed that certainly. But you did all this to good people. You cut them apart. You put chips in their heads. You made enslaved soldiers."

Eleni's smile faded.

"I created order," she corrected. "I'm sure you have a multitude of improvements because of what I did. The world runs on chaos. I designed something which could override that."

Lazer Droid clenched his fists. "Have you now."

Eleni's eyes hardened. "By giving the fallen *purpose*."

"By creating damage where there was none."

"By improving on that which could be improved."

"A job no one gave you!"

"I GAVE IT TO MYSELF!" she yelled. "When you first got your prosthetics, you were ecstatic, the speed and strength you displayed, your ability to jump higher than you ever had before! You reveled in it!"

"Only because of what I thought I had lost by consequence of my own actions to which we both know, was all a lie!"

Lazer Droid felt the air thicken.

"Eleni," Lazer Droid said quietly.

That was the first time he'd used her name.

It made her pause.

"Your system is built on control," he continued. "But control isn't strength."

Eleni's gaze narrowed. "No?"

Lazer Droid nodded once. "Control is fear."

Eleni's expression flickered.

"Why are you here?" she asked again, but sharper now. "If you wanted to kill me, you would've tried already."

"I'm not here to kill you," Lazer Droid said.

Eleni's lips parted slightly.

Surprise.

Then suspicion.

Then, slowly, understanding.

She glanced past him again.

Not at the hallway.

At the floor.

As if she was suddenly listening.

Feeling.

Vibration.

A subtle, distant hum, barely audible.

But present.

"What did you do Mr. Linard?" she asked.

Lazer Droid didn't answer.

Eleni's face tightened.

"You wouldn't," she whispered. "You can't be that reckless."

Lazer Droid stepped closer. "Reckless is what you've done to hundreds of people. I calculate multitudes of possibilities and by my most recent calculation, I am certain with one hundred percent probability, that my current decision, is the best one to make right now!"

Eleni's voice sharpened. "This building contains proprietary systems. Research. Hardware...."

"And a load of bad memories," Lazer Droid cut in.

Eleni froze.

Her eyes widened just slightly, like she was running calculations in her head and realizing the answer she didn't want.

Then her gaze snapped back to him, cold now.

"You cannot destroy Helix," she said.

Lazer Droid nodded once.

"You're probably right, but as I cancelled the company's insurance policy on the building and its contents, I can give Helix a hellified repair bill!"

Eleni's composure cracked, just a hairline fracture, but real.

Then she moved.

Fast.

She quickly pulled a laser firearm and fired at Lazer Droid as he quickly raised his right arm where a little device came out of his wrist and he fired a dart at her."

The laser went clean through his right shoulder causing him to flinch back to the right just as the dart hit her in the left side of her neck.

She started to dip backward.

Lazer Droid moved with a speed burst and caught her in a blink as she was falling.

Eleni gasped, not in pain, more in shock.

No one has ever helped her.

No one has ever had to help her.

And yet here was this man whom she had harmed in multiple ways, catching her before she hit the floor.

Eleni's eyes flared with rage.

"You arrogant son of a..."

She passed out before she could finish her sentence.

Thanks to a precise hit at the side of her neck.

A controlled shutdown.

Eleni's body went limp.

He held her there for a second.

Not because he felt mercy.

Because he understood something.

If she died in that building, she became a martyr to the loyalists who still believed in Helix.

If she lived...

she became proof Helix could be beaten.

Lazer Droid lifted her and put her over her shoulders.

Carried her.

You know she's going to try and come after you?

"Better me than others," he replied. "We'll deal with that when the time comes!"

He walked out carrying her.

***

The countdown wasn't in Lazer Droids head.

It wasn't in Crystal's voice.

It was in the building.

A subtle rhythm of vibrations.

A tightening.

A pressure.

As Lazer Droid descended the stairwell with Eleni over his shoulders, the lights flickered once.

Then again.

A distant thump trembled through the concrete.

Structural charges engaging.

He didn't run.

He moved with purpose.

Step after step.

Hallway after hallway.

Down and out.

***

The night air hit him like a wave when he exited the building.

He carried Eleni across the courtyard.

No I.C.E. agents intercepted him.

No helicopters came.

Helix truly was empty now.

Or too broken to respond.

Lazer Droid sat her in the front seat of a vehicle parked near the perimeter, one of Helix's own cars, keys still inside.

He started it.

You're gonna make it look like an accident? Crystal asked excitedly

"What's wrong with you?" he asked.

Just looking out for you.

134

"Reformat the vehicle and program for delivery to Heritages' Emergency Department. Contact them on approach!"

The blue gulf ball sized sphere exited his right shoulder and traversed to the car, transforming it into black Tesla Roadster with blue lights around the trim."

"Really?" asked Lazer Droid.

It's very rare, it'll garner more attention when she arrives at the hospital.

"Just make sure it reverts back after they get her inside."

Reversion sequence time added in!

Not far.

Not long.

Just long enough.

Then.

Behind him, the Helix Systems compound made a sound that wasn't an explosion.

It was a deep, grinding collapse.

Like a giant exhaling.

Glass shattered. Steel buckled. Concrete folded.

Helix didn't go out in flames.

It fell to dust.

Lazer Droid didn't look back for long.

"Nice!"

He only watched until he was sure it was real.

The car then took off leaving the compound as he walked to where he last left the bike.

I figured Helix didn't need the glitz or glamour of a full-blown explosion. Let them just notice it's not there anymore.

"I love how you think," he said as he leapt over the fence and as the bike decloaked.

He then hopped on the bike, revved it up and turned around one hundred and eighty degrees, and took off towards the expressway.

TWENTY-SIX

HERITAGE VALLEY HOSPITAL continued to sit on the hillside looking like a monument to control order.

The exterior was busied with the hustle of ambulance traffic, cars dropping off patients, it had been a busy night with the ruckus caused at the mall.

The windows glowed in disciplined rows, each light suggesting life, urgency, and quiet authority.

Inside, the hospital was wide awake. Polished floors reflected fluorescent lighting with surgical precision. The air smelled faintly of antiseptic and recycled ventilation. Corridors were wide, intentionally uncluttered, designed for speed and surveillance as much as care. Security cameras blended seamlessly into corners and ceiling panels, present but unobtrusive.

Eleni Kallistratos awoke under fluorescent lights, next to a drawn curtain.

The smell of antiseptic and latex.

The muted chaos of an emergency room.

Her head throbbed.

A seasoned Certified Registered Nurse Practioner leaned over her, speaking calmly, while an RN managed the IV pump in the background after starting an IV with a bolus of Normal saline.

"Ma'am? Can you hear me?"

Eleni's eyes focused slowly.

Her wrists were restrained.

Not tightly.

Just enough.

Her mouth tasted like metal.

She blinked once.
Twice.
Then her gaze sharpened.
She turned her head slightly and saw where she was.
Heritage Valley Hospital.
Eleni's expression didn't break into panic.
It didn't break into fear.
It broke into something far more dangerous.
A quiet, trembling fury.
Because for the first time in a long time...
someone had taken control away from her.
And she would live to remember it.

TWENTY-SEVEN

IN THE LINARD household, the quiet and calm was only over-shadowed by the news as Henry and Patrice watched, still in awe of all that had transpired.

"...the perpetrator, a former U. S. serviceman, Major Thomas Reddy, and who was thwarted by what looked to be a 'Power Ranger', was found still alive, but semi-conscious, with-out his arms or legs, attached. He will be transported to Har-bourview as Heritages' orthopedic surgery department is under-going an ongoing investigation related to, in fact, the abuse of prosthetic implantation found not to be needed, and the weaponizing of patients receiving those prosthetics, which was in collaboration with Helix Systems..."

As the news broadcast continued, Daryl came out of his old bedroom with a duffle bag on his back with Shadow trailing faithfully behind.

"Son they think you're a Power Ranger," laughed Henry as Patrice flagged him.

"Pay him no mind," she said as Daryl bent over and kissed her on the forehead. "You sure you don't just want to stay? With that investigation, I don't think you have anything to worry about."

"The facility may be gone, and Heritage may be monitoring their surgeons, but Helix is still out there with a network and re-sources and there are I.C.E. agents out there and I need to find them."

Henry stood up. "How will you find 'em son?"

Daryl shrugged lightly. "The ones trying to live normal lives won't cause trouble. I'm not worried about them. The ones still serving Helix?" He smiled faintly. "They'll make noise. They always do."

He shifted the bag on his shoulder. "Besides, I need to get back to work. Bills don't pay themselves."

"You can talk to machines," started Henry, "I saw a boy talk to an ATM on a T V show and it gave him money!"

"Dad," Daryl chuckled, "that's television!"

"Henry what's wrong with you," Patrice scolded.

"I'm just saying, if you askin', how's it wrong?"

Patrice sighed and changed the subject. "If you drive through Baltimore, tell Mrs. Johnson we said hello," started Patrice as Henry just shook his head.

"All them people in Baltimore," started Henry, "What makes you think he gonna run into Mrs. Johnson?"

Daryl laughed. "I can stop by and say hello to Mrs. Johnson if mom wants me too."

"What about your bike?" asked Patrice, "Your job gonna let you keep it on the truck?"

"It wouldn't be a problem, but I want to keep my identity a secret as much as possible so Crystal's gonna keep it hidden for me."

Shadow barked once as if in agreement.

Daryl knelt and scratched behind his ears. "Watch over them for me, okay?"

Shadow licked his hand.

Patrice, got up, stepped forward, and pulled Daryl into a hug that lingered a second longer than either of them expected.

"Be careful," she whispered.

Henry clapped his right hand on Daryl's shoulder. "And don't be a stranger."

"I'll call when I get settled," Daryl promised.

He took one last look around the living room, the couch, the TV, the quiet, ordinary safety of it all.

Then he opened the door and stepped out into the night.

*****

The hospital suite was quiet except for the muted voice of the news.

Eleni Kallistratos lay propped against crisp white pillows, one arm resting at her side, the other loosely draped over the blanket.

A heart monitor ticked steadily beside her, indifferent to reputation, ambition, or failure.

On the wall-mounted screen, footage looped endlessly.

...Authorities confirm the collapse of the Helix Systems facility late last night. No fatalities have been reported. Investigations are ongoing into allegations of illegal prosthetic weaponization, neural coercion, and human rights violations...

Eleni watched without blinking.

Her face was pale but composed. A faint bruise marked her neck where the dart had found its target. Otherwise, she looked untouched, too intact for someone whose empire had just been erased.

The door to her room opened softly.

Eleni didn't turn.

"You're awake," a man's voice said calmly.

She recognized it instantly.

Michael Warner stepped into the room, impeccably dressed in a tailored charcoal suit, silver at his temples, his posture relaxed in the way of someone who had never needed to hurry. He looked too refined to belong in a hospital, and far too comfortable to be a visitor.

Eleni's eyes flicked toward him at last.

"Steven Tanner," she started, "you died fourteen years ago? You're not supposed to exist."

"That's not been my name in as long a time," he replied. "And you know this, so don't get coy with me."

"What do you want now?"

He smiled faintly. "Some sort of promise of my R-O-I," he replied, spreading his hands slightly, "here we are, millions of dollars spent on your failed experiment..."

"My experiment wasn't a failure," she corrected.

"And yet, her we are," Michael crossed the room and stopped near the window, glancing briefly at the skyline beyond the glass before turning back to her.

"I watched the footage," he continued. "The building. The agents. I'm assuming the girl escaped?"

Eleni nodded.

He shook his head in the affirmative. "You lost control," he said, not accusing, merely stating fact.

"I was betrayed," Eleni replied coolly. "By variables you assured me were contained."

Michael nodded once, as if accepting a minor correction. "The world is changing faster than anticipated."

He moved closer to the bed.

"More anomalies," he went on. "More spontaneous expressions. Energy-based phenomena. Genetic awakenings. Sorcery." His gaze sharpened slightly. "People like your young captive are no longer rare."

Eleni looked back at the screen.

"And Helix?" she asked.

"Helix was a prototype," Michael said. "A proof of concept."

Her eyes snapped to him.

"You let it fall."

"I allowed it to evolve," he corrected. "And then I allowed it to fail."

Silence stretched between them.

Michael leaned forward slightly, lowering his voice.

"The mistake wasn't the technology," he said. "It was loyalty. Your I.C.E. agents were strong... but they were mismatched."

Eleni's fingers curled against the blanket.

"You built soldiers," he continued. "The world is now producing gods."

He straightened.

"We need agents who can *stand beside them*. Who can match them. Who can survive them."

Eleni searched his face. "And what is my role in this... recalibration?"

Michael's smile returned, thin, controlled.

"You don't get another failure," he said softly.

The words were gentle. The meaning was not.

"You will rebuild," he went on. "Quietly. Selectively. No grand facilities. No public infrastructure. Loyalty will be... absolute."

Eleni exhaled slowly.

"I need medical teams, technicians, resources..."

"We will work that out," he interrupted. Michael then moved within inches of her face and met her gaze without hesitation.

"Failure," he said, "is not...a career finisher, it is a spring board and we will jump higher than we have before."

He turned toward the door, then paused.

"Oh," he added casually. "Your Lazer Droid?"

Eleni stiffened.

"He's only one aspect, there are others out there and we need to get ready for them," Michael said. "So enjoy your recovery."

The door closed behind him with a soft click.

Eleni lay back against the pillows; eyes fixed on the ceiling now.

Helix was gone for now.

But the war?

The war had just learned how to adapt.

EPILOGUE

THE EXPRESSWAY UNSPOOLED ahead of him, smooth and endless.

Lazer Droid rode steady, blue light tracing the seams of his armor and the contours of the motorcycle beneath him. The glow reflected faintly off the asphalt, a quiet signature against the night as the city lights fell away and the road opened into long, unguarded miles.

Where to first? asked Crystal.

"First we go to Jersey, crash there for a couple of nights while I take my physical assessment etcetera. Then we pick up my rig and follow wherever my manifests take us."

Sounds like a plan.

Lightning flashed overhead.

Distant. Silent.

No rain followed.

He eased off the throttle.

Probability of precipitation: zero, Crystal noted.

"I know," Lazer Droid replied.

He guided the bike onto the shoulder and kicked the stand down. The engine purred once, then settled into silence as another flash split the clouds above, light without thunder, power without release.

The air shifted.

Pressure built, familiar and electric.

A controlled descent of light formed ahead of him, arcs folding inward as Kalelectra touched down on the pavement.

Energy danced briefly across her suit before dissipating, the electricity obeying her will.

Lazer Droid straightened.

"Jennifer—"

She tilted her head. "In this suit, it's *Kalelectra*."

He paused, then nodded. "Right. My mistake. Love the suit!"

"It was given to me by a dear friend!" She smiled.

He nodded.

"How's your mother?" he asked.

"She's doing well," Kalelectra said. "Rehab facility in Lafayette. The Hill at Whitemarsh. She's getting stronger every day."

"Good," he said. "I'm glad."

For a moment, they stood in companionable silence, traffic whispering past in the distance.

"Helix isn't standing anymore," Kalelectra said.

"The building isn't," Lazer Droid replied. "But they still are."

She nodded.

They spoke quietly then, about Sorrie, and what she was becoming. About Feldman disappearing into a new life with too much knowledge to ever be comfortable. About freedom, and how it didn't always arrive clean or gentle.

"There was a loyalist," Lazer Droid added. "Helix fed him upgrades and pointed him in our direction."

"Me and you?"

He nodded as he looked to the right briefly, "and Dr, Feldman!"

Kalelectra's posture stiffened. "Did you..."

"He's alive," Lazer Droid said. "But he'll never hurt anyone again."

She studied him, then accepted the answer.

"What now?" she asked.

"I get back on the road," he said. "Truck routes. City to city. Any I.C.E. agent who *chooses* to break the law will make noise. I'll find them and deal with them accordingly."

"Judge, jury, and executioner?"

"Not quite like that," started Lazer Droid, "but I'll be a fair and impartial juror."

A faint smile crossed her face. "That figures."

He hesitated. "And you?"

Kalelectra looked skyward.

"I've got a lead," she said. "Someone super-powered. Someone who never paid for crimes he committed fourteen years ago in Philadelphia."

"Where is he?" Lazer Droid asked.

"Pittsburgh area," she replied. "Somewhere out there."

Crystal's blue glow pulsed softly at Lazer Droid's shoulder.

Be careful, Kalelectra. Confirm your facts before you rush in.

"Crystal said to be careful and make sure your info is correct before getting into anything."

"You still hear her?"

"All the time," Lazer Droid said smilingly.

They stepped closer and embraced, no urgency, no fear. Just shared understanding.

Then Kalelectra stepped back.

"Don't totally disappear," she said. "You now know where I live."

"You either, stop in on my parents from time to time, they'd love to see you!"

She smiled as she rose into the sky, lightning catching her silhouette before she vanished into the clouds.

Lazer Droid watched until the night reclaimed her.

He exhaled.

You know she's going to leap before she looks, Crystal said.

"Yup," he replied.

He lifted the stand, rolled back onto the expressway, and accelerated into the dark.

The blue glow stretched forward.

And somewhere ahead, the road waited.

About the Author

Derrick J. Truesdale is a healthcare professional who spent over thirty years wanting to tell the stories he believed would both entertain and inspire. Today, those long-held ideas have become interconnected science fiction and fantasy novels that stand alone while forming a larger, evolving universe.

His worlds can be dark at times—but they are never without purpose. He writes with the hope of encouraging others to explore their imagination, embrace transformation, and discover strength in unexpected places.

Welcome to the world of Semaj, where seemingly separate stories share deeper connections waiting to be discovered

www.SemajBooks.com